DATE DUE   OCT 04

12-13-04			
5-12-05			
JUL 26 '05			
9-27-0			
9-12-0			
12-28-06			
JAN 3 1 2013			
GAYLORD			PRINTED IN U.S.A.

THE ESCHER TWIST

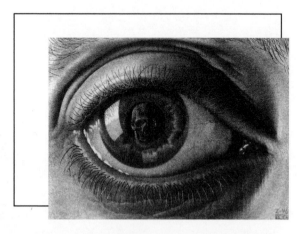

"One who watches us all"

M.C.Escher

The Escher Twist

A Homer Kelly Mystery

JANE LANGTON

BEELER LARGE PRINT
Hampton Falls, New Hampshire, 2002

Library of Congress Cataloging-in-Publication Data

Langton, Jane
    The Escher twist : A Homer Kelly mystery / Jane Langton.
    p.   cm.—(The Beeler Large Print mystery series)
ISBN 1-57490-451-5 (acid-free paper)
    1. Kelly, Homer (Fictitious character)—Fiction. 2. Escher,
M.C. (Maurits Cornelis}, 1898-1972—Exhibitions—Fiction. 3.
Cambridge (Mass.)—Fiction. 4. College teachers—Fiction. 5.
Missing persons—Fiction. 6. Large type books. I. Title. II. Series.

PS3562.A515 E8 2002b
813'.54—dc21   2002015530

Published in Large Print by arrangement with
Viking Penguin, A member of Penguin Putnam, Inc.

BEELER LARGE PRINT
is published by
Thomas T. Beeler, Publisher
Post Office Box 659
Hampton Falls, New Hampshire 03844

Typeset in 16 point Times New Roman type.
Printed on acid-free paper, sewn and bound by
Edwards Brothers in Ann Arbor, Michigan.

THE BEELER LARGE PRINT MYSTERY SERIES

Edited by Audrey A. Lesko

Also available in Large Print by Jane Langton

A FACE ON THE WALL

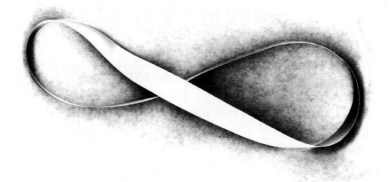

For fellow enthusiasts Andy, David, and Chris

Double Planetoid

Two regular tetrahedrons, piercing each other, float through space as a planetoid. The light-colored one is inhabited by human beings who have completely transformed their region into a complex of houses, bridges and roads. The darker tetrachedron has remained in its natural state, with rocks, on which plants and prehistoric animals live. The two bodies fit together to make a whole, but they have no knowledge of each other.

M.C. Escher

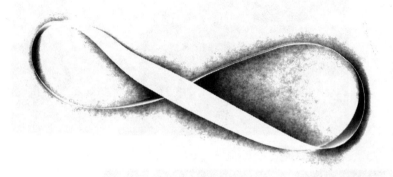

They have no knowledge of each other.

Perhaps the city of Cambridge, interpenetrated by the garden cemetery of Mount Auburn, is a double planetoid. The two parts fit together to make a whole, but the city of the living repudiates the city of the dead. As soon as breathing stops and their bodies are cold, the dead are spirited away. Only later do they turn up among the green hills of Mount Auburn as chunks of granite, stiff and upright, their speech reduced to chiseled words on their stony faces. "Hello," they say on Tuesday, "my name is Chester Smith," and on Wednesday and Thursday and forever after, only "Chester Smith."

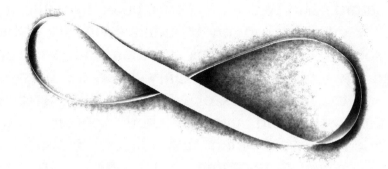

In recent years the center of Old Cambridge has become one of the liveliest, noisiest, and most crowded areas in the Boston Metropolitan District, with a proliferation of restaurants, bars, shops and boutiques, thronged with students from Harvard and thousands of other young people attracted to the street scene and the night life, along with hordes of tourists.
—*Blue Guide to Boston and Cambridge*

A FEW CURRENT RESIDENTS OF CAMBRIDGE—

Leonard Sheldrake, crystallographer, attic apartment, 24 Sibley Road. Leonard is thirty-nine.

Eloise Winthrop, Leonard's widowed landlady, 24 Sibley Road. Eloise is eighty-one.

Maud Starr, proprietor of Twice-Told Togs, Huron Avenue

Leonard Underdown, professor of geology, Massachusetts Institute of Technology

Barbara Strong, resident, Aberdeen Street Nursing Home

Edward Fell, resident, Aberdeen Street Nursing

i

Home
B. J. Larkin, landlord, 87 Sibley Road

And of course there are multitudes of others. Like most cities, Cambridge is not one metropolis but many. Its hundred-thousand multiracial inhabitants occupy every sort of dwelling, from the elegant habitations of Brattle Street and the Georgian dormitories of Harvard University to the three-deckers and comfortable Victorians of farflung neighborhoods east, west, north and south of Harvard Square.

Six-and-a-half square miles of urban density are relieved by parks and playing fields and by a famous cemetery—

Mount Auburn Cemetery was established in 1831 by Dr. Jacob Bigelow, whose intent was to create the first garden cemetery in the U.S. . . . Atop the highest hill . . . is a tower . . .
—Blue Guide to Boston and Cambridge

Therefore, in taking a proper census, what about underground residents? Shouldn't they be included in the total population by some sort of mortuary statistic? After all, there are ninety-thousand expired citizens in Mount Auburn alone, including—

Professor Zachariah Winthrop, Mrs. Winthrop's
    deceased husband, Willow Avenue
Isabella Stewart Gardner, Auburn Lake
Mary Baker Eddy, Halcyon Avenue
Harold Edgerton, Story Road
Buckminster Fuller, Bellwort Path

Henry Wadsworth Longfellow, Indian Ridge

Nathaniel Bowditch, Tulip Path

Benjamin Bates, *Founder of Cheap Postage*, Pyrola Path

Margaret Fuller Ossoli, Pyrola Path, a memorial stone

And then perhaps, by some sort of ectoplasmic reckoning, an all-inclusive census might take into account the ten billion particles of floating brain tissue sloughed off by students passing through Harvard Square—bits and pieces of spectral substance thickening the air, breathed in by all.

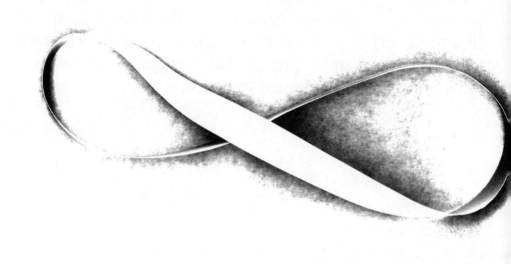

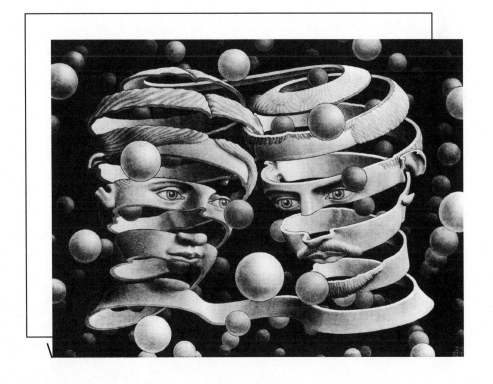

Bond of Union

The printmaker has something of the minstrel spirit; he sings, and in every print . . . he repeats his song over and over again . . . The graphic artist . . . is like a blackbird singing at the top of a tree . . . He wishes that the wind would scatter his leaves over the earth . . . not like the dry leaves of autumn, but rather like seeds ready to germinate and light as a feather.

M.C.Escher

On display in the Cambridge Gallery on Huron Avenue, prints by Dutch artist M. C. Escher. Hours 10–6 weekdays, 10–9 Saturday, 1–6 Sunday. Till July 1.
                                                  The Boston Phoenix

LOVE AT FIRST SIGHT IS FOLLY. USUALLY THE demented people come to their senses, but sometimes only when it's too late.

Frieda's and Leonard's case was typically instantaneous and ridiculous. Strangers, they met at an exhibition of the work of the Dutch printmaker M. C. Escher.

The Cambridge gallery on Huron Avenue was not far from Leonard's attic apartment on Sibley Road.

There were a lot of other people in the gallery. They kept flooding in the door, coming in from the rain, picking up the free pamphlet and walking slowly through the rooms, moving alone or in clusters, parting and rejoining.

Frieda and Leonard drifted together before a famous wood-engraving called *A Dream.* In a Gothic arcade a stone bishop lay on a sarcophagus with an enormous insect crouched upon his breast.

Leonard spoke up first. "It's more like a nightmare than a dream."

"Oh, yes," said Frieda quickly. She laughed. "And such a joke."

"Because the bug is praying. It's a praying mantis."

"Praying to the bishop."

"So much for organized religion."

They wandered together through the rest of the exhibition of Escher's prints. Leonard was familiar with all of them, in fact they were part of his life. But instead of lecturing to Frieda he said outrageous things and made her laugh.

She was puzzled by the woodcut called *Moebius Strip,* a latticed figure-eight inhabited by ants. "I just don't understand it. I mean, I've heard of Moebius strips, but I don't see what's so special about them."

"Look." Leonard took the gallery pamphlet, creased it sharply and tore off one edge. "You make a twist like this, then stick the ends together to make a loop. See?"

He held the strip together with finger and thumb, then made a magical gesture with the other hand. "Presto, behold the impossible. Before the twist there were two sides. Now—here, try it. Run your finger all the way around."

"Oh," said Frieda, "it goes inside and outside."

"So there's only one surface now, not two."

She laughed. "It's bewitched."

There were only forty prints in the exhibition, but they took their time. Stopping before the last one, Leonard looked at Frieda and introduced himself. "Leonard. I'm a geologist. Well, actually I'm a crystallographer."

At once her cheerfulness faded, and she glanced away. "My name's Frieda. I'm an artist."

Words welled up in Leonard, questions that would have been intrusive if they weren't suddenly so important. *Where do you live? How could there be someone like you?* "Are you a printmaker like Escher?"

"No, no." She looked across the room as if searching for someone. She seemed embarrassed. "I make drawings. Faces, portraits of people."

They turned back to the picture, a lithograph called *Bond of Union*. The heads of a man and woman floated in space, joined together at top and bottom like strips of a peeled orange.

Leonard said calmly, "That's you and me."

It was clear that he meant it. "You don't know me," murmured Frieda. Her jauntiness was gone.

"I know all I need to know," said Leonard. "Except—oh, well, I suppose you're married."

"No. My husband died last year."

Leonard tried to hide his pleasure. "You're very young to be a widow."

"Yes, I am." Frieda made a lame joke of being pitiful. "And I was very young to be an orphan. And very much too young to be—" She broke off.

Leonard couldn't help himself. "To be what?"

"I'm sorry." Frieda turned and walked quickly away.

Was she crying? After a moment Leonard followed her out into the hall and waited, keeping an eye on the door where women went in and out.

He waited and waited, but she didn't appear. He spoke to the man at the desk. "Did a woman in a green coat leave just now?"

"You mean two women together?"

"Two women? I don't think so."

"Well, two women in green coats left a minute ago."

Leonard waited a little longer, surprised at the keenness of his disappointment. He didn't even know Frieda's last name.

People came and went. Some of them signed the visitors' book.

The visitors' book—Leonard crossed the hall and looked at it. There were only a few names on the page for today—

Max Rubin, Cambridge
Helen Crowley, Medfield
Mr. and Mrs. Charles Spratt, Weston
Tyler Biggy, Somerville
Isaac and Marilynne Jacob, Cambridge

Frieda was not there.

Dispirited, Leonard wrapped his checkered scarf closely around his neck and left the gallery, furious with himself. He found Huron Avenue blocked by a jack-knifed truck. Cars were backing up, honking, edging around the obstruction and zooming forward in plunging splashes of foam. A few pedestrians shuffled along the sidewalk, crouching under umbrellas. One of the umbrellas blew inside-out.

There was no sign of Frieda in her green coat.

<hr>

2

TEN MINUTES LATER THERE WERE A FEW MORE NAMES in the visitors' book, including

Mary and Homer Kelly, Concord

"You see, Homer," said Mary, urging him along into the first room in the gallery, "this is why we need to move to Cambridge. Cultural events like this."

"What about the river?" said Homer grumpily. "The river's a cultural event. It goes on all the time."

"Oh, Homer, you can't possibly miss the river. Think of last February! Remember how often we had to make

4

four tries to get a car up that icy river bank?"

"Well, that's true," admitted Homer. He cheered up. "Say, look at that. A Moebius strip. Look at the way it twists around on itself. See?"

"Twists around on itself?"

"Don't you know about Moebius strips? Good grief, Mary Kelly, I thought you were an educated woman. Wait a sec. I'll show you how they work."

Homer pawed in his pocket, extracted a Cambridge parking ticket, tore a strip off the edge and demonstrated the strange properties of a Moebius strip.

"Good heavens," said Mary. "How can there be such a thing?"

"Don't we look like twins in our green coats?"

"Won't you take yours off and stay awhile—Cousin Kitty?"

"No, no, I have to go. That button, dear. Your coat has lost a button. Where is it? You should sew it back on."

"It fell off somewhere. It doesn't matter."

"Tell me, dear, who was that? That man you were talking to?"

"In the gallery? His name's Leonard. He's a crystallographer."

"Leonard what?"

"I don't know."

"Well, it's too bad. You know, dear, you've got to take an interest. It's been a year now since Tom died. I thought this man looked quite nice. He's a good deal older than you, I think, but then you're not getting any younger. Did you like him?"

"Yes, I did," said Frieda impulsively. She looked defiant. "I liked him very much."

"Well, then, why didn't you—? Do you know where he lives?"

"No, I told you. I don't know anything about him."

Kitty said goodbye, and went away satisfied. This little romance was going nowhere. And the girl was so plain. It was a wonder she'd landed a husband at all. That little episode had been an unexpected blow.

Downstairs Kitty paused as the landlord came banging in from outdoors and shook out his umbrella, flinging raindrops in all directions. At once his wife popped out into the hall and said tartly, "There's some woman on the phone."

"Oh?" The landlord grinned, pulled off his sopping raincoat and hurried into the apartment. His wife slammed the door behind him with great force.

Kitty shuddered, then turned to the mirror on the wall beside Mr. Larkin's door and smiled at her reflection. If she and Frieda were twins in their green coats, it was obvious which was the pretty one.

Left alone upstairs, Frieda looked out the window at the homely three-deckers on the other side of the street. The pavement was shining, the parked cars gleamed, rainwater dripped from the chainlink fence.

She took a sheet of paper from her work table and cut a long narrow piece with a pair of scissors. Then she twisted it and taped the ends together.

There, look at that—it was a Moebius strip, just like Leonard's.

LEONARD SHELDRAKE HAD FOUND A PROBLEM FOR HIS students in Elementary Crystallography—

There was once a king with five sons. In his will he ordered his kingdom to be divided among them into five regions, each bounded by the other four. Can the terms of the will be satisfied?

The problem had been posed in the year 1840 by mathematician August Ferdinand Moebius. Leonard made twenty-three copies and slapped them into a folder. Then he walked to the window, stepping carefully around the bucket that was collecting drips of rain from a leak in the roof.

The storm was over and the sun was out, going down in a flare of red above the splendid chimneys of the house next door. Leonard enjoyed the way the complex rooftops of the houses on Sibley Road had classic crystalline shapes—they were cuboid, pyramidal, prismatic. He watched as a ragged flight of birds burst into view, flapping hard and fast in the direction of the sunset. *Like volunteer firemen,* thought Leonard, *pulling on their pants and racing to a conflagration on the western horizon.*

It occurred to him that the sun was setting right now over the entire eastern seaboard of the United States, including the unknown place where the woman called Frieda was standing at this moment, or sitting or walking or talking or eating or sleeping.

There was a draft around the frame of the window. Leonard stuffed the gap with a sock.

He didn't mind the bucket and the sock. He felt lucky

to have stumbled on this place. The house was rundown, but it had an august address. Sibley Road and the parallel streets between Huron Avenue and Brattle were part of the most fashionable neighborhood in the city of Cambridge.

The privilege of living here had been like a Boy Scout's reward. He had helped an old woman cross the street.

There she had been, old Mrs. Winthrop, frozen with fear in the middle of the dangerous intersection of Brattle Street and Fresh Pond Parkway, with cars honking at her from three directions. Leonard had run out and helped her to the sidewalk, and then because she had seemed so feeble he had walked her home, helped her up the porch steps and saved her from tripping over the head of a wild beast as she stepped into her front hall.

The head was attached to a tigerskin rug. "Oh, dear," whispered the old lady. "I always forget." She sagged against a totem pole.

Leonard was charmed by the clutter of objects in the dark entry. Spears and primitive musical instruments hung from the ceiling. There was a shimmer of gleaming brass—a hookah, huge trays from Benares. Politely he said, "Wouldn't you like to sit down?"

"No, no, I'm quite all right." The old woman's cheeks were no longer gray with fatigue. She stood upright and beamed at him. "I want to show you something."

Taking his arm she led him across the hall and pointed to a framed photograph on the wall above a bulky handplow from Azerbaijan. "My husband Zachariah among the Zulus."

Leonard looked respectfully at the painted tribesmen and the imposing figure of a bearded white man. He had

8

seen the picture before. It celebrated some important moment in anthropological history.

Struck by an idea, he turned to her. "Oh, ma'am, I don't suppose you have a room for rent?"

Her rosy face fell, and she shook her head sadly. "Oh, dear me, no. I'm terribly sorry."

And Leonard had murmured, "Well, never mind," and thanked her, and opened the front door and closed it behind him and started down the porch steps.

But then she had opened the door and called after him, "Well, of course there's the attic!"

A stellar dodecahedron is placed in the center and is enclosed by a translucent sphere like a soap bubble. This symbol of order and beauty reflects the chaos in the shape of a heterogeneous collection of all sorts of useless, broken and crumpled objects.

M.C. Escher

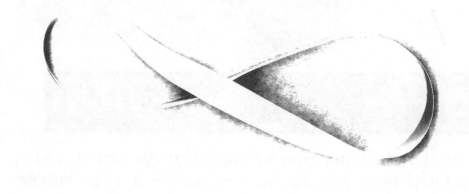

SO LEONARD HAD MOVED HAPPILY INTO THE ATTIC, and at once the pleasant regular pattern of life in Mrs. Winthrop's house had begun. The attic radiators shuddered, the wiring sizzled and sparked and the bathroom should have been removed to a museum, but he was grateful to be Mrs. Winthrop's tenant. He didn't mind the ancient plumbing. In fact he delighted in the Escher-like pattern of the water glugging slowly down the drain of the venerable bathtub. Did it swirl the other way in the southern hemisphere? Did the rotation of the earth create pairs of spirals twisting oppositely above and below the equator, glugging left or right down a billion different drains?

Nor did he mind the shabbiness of the large house and the disshevelment of the neglected garden. Undoubtedly Mrs. Winthrop's property was an eyesore to the neighbors, whose large houses were smartly painted, whose gardens sported ecstasies of trellised fencing, frolicsome teahouses and peekaboo garden gates. No truckload of bark mulch had ever been dumped in her back yard, no carpet-lengths of grass unrolled across her weedy lawn.

He guessed that Mrs. Winthrop's dignity was bound up with her house, but it was clear that the loving identity between them had nothing to do with contemporary fashions in remodelling or the design of formal gardens.

Leonard knew little about his elderly landlady except that she was the widow of that famous old anthropologist Zachariah Winthrop. It was clear, too, that her devotion to her husband's memory was untiring, although he had been dead for years.

The house was large. Leonard and Mrs. Winthrop lived apart. His attic had once been the servants' quarters, and it was therefore entirely separate. His back stairway plunged straight down to the rear door. His friends could come and go without encountering the mistress of 24 Sibley Road.

One of his friends, unfortunately, was that nutty woman Judy Plumrose, who had bounced noisily up the back stairs, flung open the attic door and cried, "Oo, what have we here?" And moved right in.

It had taken him three weeks of argument and a messy confrontation before she moved out again, before peace descended once more on Leonard's eyrie at the top of the house.

The contrast between before-Judy and after-Judy reminded him of an Escher print—but then everything reminded Leonard of an Escher print. This one was *Order and Chaos.*

Judy had been the broken things around the edge of the picture—the bits of string, the broken bottle, the crumpled piece of paper—while the beautiful order that had returned to his life was the starry crystal in the center.

The crystal in the center—Leonard prepared his lectures, he went to and from his classes and spent many hours at his desk working on his paper for the Mineralogical Society of America, *Anti-symmetry in the Prints of M. C. Escher*—but he had come to feel more and more enclosed in a kind of crystalline perfection, as though the screen of his computer were itself a crystal and so was his shoddy neglected attic at the top of Mrs.

Winthrop's house. The peaked roof with its projecting gables was like the semi-regular polyhedrons crowning the towers of Escher's famous lithograph, *The Waterfall.*

He was a crystal living inside a crystal. Everything in Leonard's life seemed regulated by the fundamental operations of crystallography—translation, rotation and reflection—the three rules that had so fascinated M. C. Escher. On Leonard's desk the books were at right angles to his notebook and parallel to his pens and pencils. *The eraser is out of line. Turn it a few degrees.*

Now, however, after yesterday's tour of the Escher exhibition, his perfectly regulated life had been smashed for a second time by the woman in the green coat.

Leonard groaned, pushed aside his stack of pages and rubbed his bristling chin. He needed a shave. Scraping back his chair, he walked into the bathroom and looked at himself in the mirror.

What had she thought of this ugly face? Obviously not much. Leonard turned roughly away from the mirror and went back to his desk. He would write her a letter.

Of course it was impossible, because he didn't know her last name nor where she lived.

Perhaps, he thought, taking up an envelope, she dwelt in Escher space, behind the door of the mill where the water went both up and down, or at the top of the upsidedown staircase, or in the bellchamber of the cathedral that rose from the sea.

Dreamily he invented a fantastic postal destination—

Ms. Frieda X
The Chessboard Town
If undeliverable at this address please forward to—

15

The Tower of Babel

or try—

The Intersected City

Writing a letter to a woman without an earthly address was like writing to John Keats. What mailman would deliver it?

Dear Frieda, wrote Leonard, beginning anyway.

But when he went out of the house half an hour later, it was not to mail his impossible letter. He was heading for the laundromat on Huron Av with a bundle of dirty clothes. From there he could walk to work.

Without a thought for his landlady Leonard ran downstairs and turned his back on her kitchen door with its tacked-up paper sign, *Mrs. Zachariah Winthrop.*

As he ambled toward the street he was not aware that she was looking out at him from behind the curtain of her dining room window. Whenever Mrs. Winthrop heard Leonard's footsteps on the stairs she hoped he would knock and come in, but he never did.

Even on the first of the month when the rent was due, he merely slipped the check under the door.

5

YOU'RE GOING TO LIKE THIS, HOMER. YOU'RE REALLY going to like the Peabody Museum."

"Well, of course I will. I told you, I've been here before."

"But did you see the glass flowers? I mean, did you really *look* at the glass flowers?"

Homer pulled the door open and said sarcastically, "I

16

assume the rays of light from the glass flowers managed to stagger up to my eyes."

Mary dodged ahead of him into the entrance hall. "It's just that I really want you to see how good it will be, living so close to all this wonderful stuff. And it will be so convenient to visit Barbara in her nursing home without driving for half an hour."

"Barbara? Oh, right, your old school friend." Glumly Homer followed his wife up the stairs to the third floor. Gloomily he inspected the cases of botanical specimens miraculously crafted in glass. "Right, right, I saw all these things before."

Mary took his arm and propelled him into the next room. "Hey, I don't remember this. Look, Homer, it's full of crystals."

Homer looked around doubtfully. The exhibition space for Harvard's collection of mineralogical and crystallogical specimens was very large.

They had the room almost to themselves. There was only one other visitor.

A gray-haired man in a checkered scarf stood in front of one of the vertical cases, scribbling in a notebook. Turning, he saw them and spoke up. "Start over here. This is the beginning."

Obediently they joined him, and he explained, "These are the native elements."

Homer stared at the immense gold nugget. "Native elements?"

"From the periodic table of elements. Gold, silver, copper and so on." He nodded and moved away.

Mary was charmed. "It's like M. C. Escher," she murmured. "This whole room. I wish he could have seen it."

At once the man in the checkered scarf came hurrying

back. "Escher? Right, you're right. But perhaps he did see it. He was here in Cambridge several times."

"Really?" said Homer, beaming. "You're another Escher enthusiast?"

Leonard laughed. "An enthusiast? Good god, I'm an Escher freak from way back." He held out his hand and introduced himself. "Leonard Sheldrake. I'm a crystallographer. I use his stuff in the courses I teach."

"No kidding," said Homer. "Well, we teach here too. Homer and Mary Kelly, bunch of courses in American Lit. Educational meatgrinder."

"Not *the* Homer Kelly? You're the big detective?"

Homer was hugely pleased, but he said, "Aw shucks."

Mary gently changed the subject. "You see, we just discovered Escher. There's an exhibition on Huron Avenue. We saw it yesterday."

"Yesterday! Well, my god, I was there yesterday too. I live just around the corner." Leonard Sheldrake paused and stared at them, and his face turned red. "You didn't happen to see a woman in a green coat?"

"A green coat?" Mary shook her head. "I don't think so. Did you, Homer?"

Homer wasn't listening. "That crazy Escher. Those upside-down, inside-out staircases, those Moebius strips, those little men going up and down forever."

"No," said Mary. "I'm afraid we didn't see her. I'm sorry."

Leonard shrugged his shoulders, and Homer eagerly blundered on. "Crystals? What did Escher have to do with crystals?"

Recovering, Leonard explained. "You may have seen them in his pictures—tetrahedrons, octahedrons, dodecahedrons, and so on. But the ones we crystallographers care about are the prints that show the

18

regular divisions of the plane—fishes and birds fitting together, swans going one way and fitting exactly with swans going the other way. He was crazy about that."

They moved on to the next group of crystals, an array of minerals identified as SULFIDES. "Yes, I remember prints like that," said Mary, staring at the crisscrossing sticks of stibnite. "I didn't think they were very interesting. Clever, but surely it isn't difficult to fit birds and fishes together?"

"Oh, but it's the *way* they're fitted together." To Mary's astonishment, Leonard Sheldrake was waxing enthusiastic. So of course was Homer. Soon the two of them were moving excitedly from case to case while Leonard talked about lattices and grids, glide reflections and sixfold rotations, vertical translations and the interdiffusion of atoms. His arms whirled in the air, making airy shapes, chopping off the corners of a cube to make an octahedron.

Mary followed along gratefully, half listening, half admiring the translucent green chunk of fluorite from Namibia, the giant spray of gypsum crystals from Mexico, the amethyst-packed caves of a geode from Brazil.

Parting at last, Leonard said, "I'm going back there tomorrow. To the Escher exhibition, I mean. Would you like to join me? Then I could explain about—"

Mary and Homer agreed at once, and Leonard went away smiling.

It had occurred to him that Frieda might have visited the gallery yesterday because she lived nearby. In that case she might come again. He vowed to drop in every day and ask about the woman in the green coat.

He had forgotten that there had been two women in green coats. He did not wonder about the other.

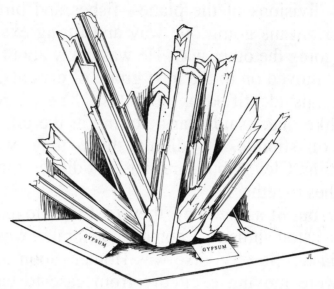

Long before there were people on the earth, crystals were already growing in the earth's crust.

M. C. Escher

6

IN HER CONDOMINIUM APARTMENT IN WATERTOWN A dreaming woman woke up, opened her eyes, then closed them again. She did not want to get up and face her sixty-third birthday. It was too horrible. No one must know.

But the fact of her birthday was not the first thing she thought of on waking. As usual, it was her loss, the memory of the terrible thing that had been done to her. She had borne her grudge for twelve long years. She would bear it for the rest of her life.

And she intended to live a long, long time.

For a few minutes longer she would rest in the delicious comfort of her bed. Feeling slightly tired of lying on her right side, she rolled over and sank into the downy softness of the pillow on her left side. She did not consciously know it, she did not say it to herself, but it was her greatest joy.

But, oh God, it was time to get up, she must get up.

It took an act of courage to lift her head from the bosomy comfort of the pillow. With a wrench she pushed back the tender blankets and struggled to sit up. Then she turned slowly until her legs were over the side.

There she sat for a moment, her head drooping, while the room tipped and whirled. Dizzily she gazed at the middle of the whirl where her breasts rose white and round under the lace of her nightgown.

The sight of her two prize possessions gave her courage. When the walls and windows stopped rocking, she pushed her fists down on the mattress and heaved herself upright.

For the first few steps she supported herself by grasping the doorframe. Then at last she could make her stumbling way to the bathroom.

She felt better after breakfast, perfectly able to walk without stooping or faltering, almost like a young woman again. Now she could do her exercises, although she detested them.

Drooping, she let her upper body fall. Hanging for a moment with her fingers touching her toes, she thought once more about the terrible thing that had been done to her. Rising again she threw her hands over her head, then let them fall and touch her toes.

For five long minutes she carried on—bending, falling, touching, rising, reaching, bending, falling, touching, rising, reaching, bending, falling—falling, falling, falling, remembering her grudge.

It was the engine that drove her.

21

She was certainly insane, the old woman, but in a particular way. Her madness was a fixation on too few things, not the healthy jumble of daily life but an alternation of obsessed attention from one thing to a second thing, then back to the first thing, then a manic return to the second thing, and once again back to the first—a loop that ran around and around and met itself, ceaselessly and without end.

7

FOR ELOISE WINTHROP ALSO, GETTING OUT OF BED IN the morning was an act of courage.

The widow of the great Zachariah Winthrop was sometimes so cramped and stiff, she doubted her strength to walk to the cemetery to visit Zach's grave.

But she too had a ruling passion. Her entire life was dedicated to her husband's memory. She *must not* be too tired. She *must* go. Zach would be expecting her. If she didn't come, he would be so disappointed.

Of course if anyone had asked Mrs. Winthrop about the metaphysical, philosophical, cosmological and theological reasons for her conviction that she was still somehow comfortably in touch with her late husband, she would have been unable to reply. Oh, she knew perfectly well in the soft fissures of her brain that it was impossible. But she was not consulting her brain.

Eloise had never been a clever woman. It was her heart, she told herself, that had guided her in all things. Zach had understood her perfectly. He had never asked for witty conversation, he had never expected her to understand anything about social anthropology. He had loved her, Eloise knew, for herself.

It was wonderful the way he had not simply vanished, like someone who has gone away and will never come back. He was very near. He had merely crossed the bridge to the other side.

Today Eloise decided to wait until after lunch to go to the cemetery. She always felt perkier after lunch. But when she heard Leonard hurry down the back stairs she pulled herself together, snatched up the *Boston Globe* and pulled open the door to the back hall, hoping to catch him for a cheery greeting, perhaps a comment about the lovely day.

But her tenant was already turning out of the driveway on his bicycle and spinning away around the corner.

Ah, well. Eloise tucked the *Globe* under her arm and set off, her big sneakers tramping solidly along the sidewalk. She wasn't even fazed by the terrible intersection of Brattle Street with Fresh Pond Parkway. When the light said WALK, she walked. The furious traffic, every fuming motorist and impatient truckdriver, had to wait while she made her slow way across.

And of course the walk was good for her old bones. Mount Auburn was so close—just a short stroll down Brattle Street to the great Egyptian gate, and then along the dear familiar ways to Zach's neighborhood on Willow Avenue.

Spring had come at last. Daffodils were blooming along all the paths in the cemetery, and everything was green. She could spread her blanket on the grass and feel Zach's presence at her side.

Eloise loved this pleasant bower. There were kindly neighbors all around, and they seemed to lean so near. Most had been old when they passed on, but some had been young, like the daughters of Thomas and Maria Curtis, two dear young women who had died in childbirth, Ellen Elizabeth and Ann Maria.

James Curtis was young too—*lost at sea on his passage from London to Charleston, South Carolina, Dec. 9, 1845, aged 25 years.*

Willow Avenue made a loop with a little neck of land in the middle. Here there was a lovely Grecian temple for the Lowell family, and a truly magnificent monument like a sofa crowned with an urn. The oddest monument was a tall triangle with the simple inscription MOUNTFORT. It was like a trumpet blast or a noble name in a Shakespeare play.

The weather was so warm, the spring day so enchanting, Mrs. Winthrop decided to go exploring, because one always came upon the most delightful people.

On Trefoil Path, for instance, she would find Joshua Stetson's gravestone with its lovely angel. It always amused Eloise to imagine that he had been buried in a ten-gallon hat.

On Bellwort Path no imagination was necessary to picture Captain Thomas Cunningham, because his tall stone was adorned with a bronze portrait. Captain Cunningham had been a bluff and stalwart-looking man, handsome and bewhiskered, just the sort of person to rely on in a crisis.

Mrs. Winthrop's favorite monument was the obelisk belonging to Barnabas Bates, THE FOUNDER OF CHEAP POSTAGE. If only Mr. Bates were postmaster general right now!

Even closer to Zachariah's neighborhood on Willow Avenue was Auburn Lake. It was just a pretty ramble along Walnut Avenue or sometimes (when Eloise was feeling frisky) a scramble down Oxalis Path.

The lake was charming with its little bridge and with the splendid row of hillside tombs along the shore. They belonged to some of Boston's best families—Lodges and Cabots, Kirklands and Higginsons. The most distinguished was the mausoleum of the Gardner family.

Eloise was proud of the fact that her very own mother had been invited to a garden party by Isabella Stewart Gardner. There had been Japanese lanterns and exquisite sandwiches—Mother had slipped a few of the delicate triangles into her pocketbook.

There were flowers everywhere. The cemetery was a riot of pink and white dogwood trees, orange azaleas and tulips in a hundred dazzling colors. Eloise was pleased to see how many visitors had come to see the blossoming of spring at Mount Auburn.

Hurrying back to Zach, she spread her scarf on the grass, settled down, opened the *Globe* to the obituary page and read some of the death notices aloud—

BELMONT
Sampson, Louisa B.
BROOKLINE
Otto, Caspar
Wilberforce, William
CAMBRIDGE
Balski, Mary
Peeps, Pearl
Galenowitz, Albert
Morton, Margaret T.

"Nobody we know today, dear," Somehow it was always a little disappointing. Eloise couldn't help wishing that one day an old friend would cross the bridge and move into this delightful neighborhood.

Putting the paper aside, she craned her neck and looked down the slope to Narcissus Path. Why, goodness, there was the bereaved mother again, tending the grave of her infant child. Such a tragedy! Dead at fourteen months!

The little boy had died twelve long years ago, and yet the grieving mother still came once a week with flowers and scattered them around the pitiful little stone. Today, good gracious, she was lying down on the mossy bank and closing her eyes. Was she taking a nap? Oh, goodness—Eloise uttered a little shriek—what was that?

A large dark form was stalking along Narcissus Path between the little boy's grave and the blocky monument celebrating deceased members of the Pond family.

A bird, it was a large bird. Not a pheasant, not a goose. What was it?

Eloise held her breath, then gave a little sigh of rapture. The bird had turned toward the sunlight and at once its breast was iridescent, shining with feathers of blue and green and gold.

It was a peacock! Oh, if only it would spread its tail!

8

THE COURAGE OF THE ELDERLY ON WAKING IN THE morning—no one needed it more than Edward, one of the senile residents of the Aberdeen Street Nursing Home.

Opening his eyes, he was always bewildered. His brain was tangled, and yet he had a profound awareness of the pity of his condition. He was bereft.

Looking around the room, he knew he had seen it before. He groaned. His sheets were drenched.

There was a lump in the bed across the room. The lump sat up. It swung its legs over the side of the bed and rubbed its frowzy hair.

Edward watched the other man dress himself. It was a long struggle. When the man finished puzzling over the buttons on his shirt he stared doubtfully at his shoes, then put one on the wrong foot.

A woman came in, said good morning to the other man, took off his shoe and fitted it on the other foot. Then she put on the other shoe and tied them both smartly. Standing, she fastened his red suspenders, talking cheerfully.

When the man in the suspenders vanished, Edward lifted his head and made whimpering noises. At once the nurse crossed the room and her face grew enormous. She was bending over him and smiling. She said, "Good morning, Edward. I'm Dorothy, remember?"

"Yes," said Edward. And he remembered that he liked her.

"It's Friday, Edward. Your niece will be coming to see you this afternoon."

Edward frowned. "I don't have a niece."

"Of course you do."

"No," said Edward crossly. He reared up from his pillow. "I tell you, I don't have any goddamn niece."

"It's all right, Edward. Here, just roll over and let me change you."

A little later Dorothy pushed his wheelchair along the corridor to the elevator, and they went down together to the first floor for breakfast.

In the dining room Edward faintly recognized the other people at his table, but he could remember only

27

one of their names, because she was the only one who talked to him.

"Barbara," he said.

"Good morning, Edward," said Barbara, with a broad smile on her clever face.

9

LEONARD WAS ON HIS WAY TO A STORE HE USUALLY avoided, the trendy little grocery on the corner of Huron and Lakeview. Most of its customers were Mrs. Winthrop's neighbors, prosperous people who lived in the happy daylight sunshine of Escher's woodcut *Day and Night.*

Few came from the other side of Huron Av, a neighborhood more like Escher's darker city—not that those three-deckers and elderly wooden arks were so bad. Canny realtors were already roaming the streets, appraising properties, their eyes alight.

Leonard would not have come here at all if he hadn't run out of coffee. On his last expedition to the supermarket he had forgotten to put it on the list. He promised himself to buy only a few beans of Mocha-Java and get out of there fast, without a glance at the croissants or the baby spinach.

But as he strode along the sidewalk on Huron Av, three amazing things happened.

The first was not really so amazing, but Leonard always enjoyed the awareness of something moving high over his head. It was the fat sausage of the Goodyear blimp, making its lazy way over the city of Cambridge. The blimp looked like one of Escher's fish shapes, and like so many of his prints it seemed slightly miraculous.

The second thing was indeed amazing, at least until Leonard thought about it afterward. It was an encounter with himself. Coming toward him along the sidewalk was a mirror image of Leonard Sheldrake. It had the same grey-streaked hair, the same clumsy arrangement of features and the same skinny shoulders. Even its windbreaker might have come from the same sporty catalog.

Leonard's mirror image seemed startled too. For an embarrassed fraction of a second their eyes met as they passed each other, separated by two feet of empty air. A few yards farther along the sidewalk Leonard looked back. His image was looking back too, in perfect obedience to the optical laws of reflection.

Leonard turned away smiling, remembering an insane moment in a Marx Brothers movie, Harpo pretending to be Chico's reflection in a nonexistent mirror.

It was just a coincidence, naturally. The other guy wasn't really an identical twin. He was a little taller than Leonard and probably twenty-five pounds heavier. Strange that it didn't happen more often. With six billion people on the planet there couldn't possibly be six billion different combinations of noses, ears and elbows. There were probably a thousand Leonard look-alikes in the state of Massachusetts.

But for a moment he had felt eerily like part of the Escher print called *Magic Mirror*. What if he and the other guy had exchanged selves? What if they had both gone through the enchanted surface and come out on the other side? What if Leonard was now the other guy, and the other guy was Leonard?

The fact that he knew everything about himself didn't

mean a thing, because perhaps until the moment of meeting he had known everything about being the other person and the other one had known everything about being Leonard.

He gave up, cast one more glance over his shoulder just as, naturally, the other guy was glancing over *his* shoulder, and walked on in the direction of coffee.

The third amazing thing was of more consequence.

10

LIKE ELOISE WINTHROP, MAUD STARR MADE A HABIT of reading the obituaries in the *Boston Globe*. Maud was the proprietor of Twice-Told Togs, an upmarket used-clothing store on Huron Avenue.

Her interest in the death notices was different from Mrs. Winthrop's. Maud read them vulture-fashion, hovering over the recently deceased, flapping back and forth to snatch at likely prey. This morning she pounced on a juicy one—

EFFINGTON—Entered into rest, April 17, Martha (Goldberg) Effington, 49, late of West Newton and Chatham. Beloved wife of Benjamin Effington. Devoted mother of—

Well, well! Poor dear Martha, may she rest in peace! The dear dead thing was only forty-nine! Her grieving husband was probably about the same age, perfect, ripe for the taking. Rich, no doubt, with a summer home on the Cape.

Maud whipped out the phone book to look up

Effington. As she ran her finger down the page, the phone rang.

It was her friend Sally, proprietor of a similar shop in Dedham. Maud and Sally were often in touch, comparing notes. Sally had just bought a darling antique wedding dress from the nineteen-thirties. "Pink satin, with posies on the shoulders and a train. *Sweet.* What about you? Got anything new?"

"*Do I!* Oh, Sally, remember that green coat with the missing button? Well, I found a button that more or less matched, so I sewed it on and then I put the coat in the window along with the green feather boa and that kooky green satin two-piece, and guess what? A guy came in, all serious—you know, his eyes bulging out of his head—and wanted to know where it came from. And so—"

"Where what came from? Maud, slow down."

"Oh, sorry, it was the coat. He wanted to know where I got the green coat. Well, of course I didn't know who brought it in. It was just draped over the doorknob a few days ago when I opened the shop."

"How strange."

"Strange? You bet it was strange. *Mysterious.* When I told this guy I didn't know, he said, 'How much?' and naturally I named a high price, but he didn't boggle, he just snatched out his billfold and handed over the cash and walked off with it. And you know what? He was holding it sort of *tenderly.* I'll bet it belongs to the woman he loves, don't you think so? Only maybe she's left him?"

"Oh, my God, Maud, maybe he's a stalker."

"A stalker? Do you really think so?"

Maud did not tell her friend Sally that she herself had been the stalker in this case. No sooner had Leonard left the shop with the coat over his arm than she had

31

whisked out her BACK SOON sign, hung it on the door, locked up and hurried after the interesting stranger with the haunted face. Did he live nearby?

You couldn't wait around for the men in your life to appear. You had to be pro-active. You had to snatch at the least opportunity.

The coat was Leonard's first piece of luck. For the last week he had spent his spare time wandering fecklessly around the neighborhood, up and down Sibley Road and Fayerweather Street and Lakeview Avenue, exploring the streets below Huron, and then moving east to Concord Avenue and Garden Street. He had visited the art gallery again and again. So far he had not caught a glimpse of the elusive Frieda.

But he had recognized the coat at once in the window of Twice-Told Togs. One of the buttons didn't match the rest, and Leonard remembered with a rush of excitement the missing button on Frieda's coat. This was her coat, it was certainly her coat. Why had she parted with it?

Climbing the hill on Sibley Road with the coat over his arm, Leonard heard footsteps clattering behind him. He stood aside to let the woman pass.

But she stopped, breathing hard. It was the woman from the shop.

"Oh, hello," she said. "It's just my morning run." Gasping, she waved a vague hand in the direction of Brattle Street, Mount Auburn Hospital, Memorial Drive and the Charles River. "I always run around the neighborhood at this time of day."

"Well, carry on," murmured Leonard, politely not looking down at her four-inch heels.

"Too exhausted," she said, grinning at him. "Do you

live around here?"

The woman looked a little sinister. Maud was wearing one of her newfound treasures, a slinky outfit with a pattern of green scales. Leonard nodded and started to walk on.

Undiscouraged, Maud teetered along beside him to the front walk of Mrs. Winthrop's house. There he nodded at her again and said, "Well, so long."

"My name's Maud," she said, looking at him eagerly.

"Leonard," mumbled Leonard, walking quickly away.

Maud stared at the house number, and at last withdrew. She could think of a dozen ways to pursue this promising beginning.

Gently Leonard laid the coat on his bed and inspected it carefully, looking for some sort of identification, remembering the way his mother embroidered her telephone number on the fabric of her umbrellas.

There was nothing personal in Frieda's coat. The pockets were empty. But when he lifted it from the bed he noticed a bulge on one side. There was an inner pocket with something in it. Leonard found the pocket and pulled out the contents.

It was an old-fashioned videocassette.

He didn't have time to set up his old VCR and look at it now. Hastily Leonard thrust the cassette into a drawer and hung the coat carefully in the closet, where it made a bright splash of green among his dun-colored clothes.

11

THE ABERDEEN STREET NURSING HOME WAS NOT THE most luxurious nursing home in Cambridge. Mary

Kelly's friend Barbara Strong had chosen it partly because it would take a little longer here to spend down her savings, but mostly because the staff had a good reputation.

Barbara was not senile, but she was so crippled by arthritis that she had institutionalized herself. Sensibly, wretchedly, she had left behind everything that had been precious in her life—her house, her garden, her pleasant town of Concord and all her friends.

Some of the friends visited her once and never came again. Others came often, bringing news and gossip, books and conversation. They ran errands for Barbara, brought her home to dinner, took her to the movies. They made friends with the wordless old women in the nursing home—Jenny, Wilma, Shirley—and the pitiful old men—Edward, Henry, Bob.

Mary Kelly was one of Barbara's loyal friends. Last week she had brought wild flags yanked up from the muddy shallows of the Sudbury River. Today she brought only herself. She wheeled Barbara out of her room and along the corridor to the place where the old men and women sat in a row against the wall. Then she pulled up a chair beside Barbara and read her a letter from their friend in Tallahassee.

Other visitors came. One was Jenny's granddaughter, bringing her baby boy to see his great-grandmother.

Babies were a rare sight in the nursing home. All the old women smiled and leaned forward to see the little darling.

Another visitor, a good-looking blond woman, admired the baby too. She held out her arms and said, "Oh, please, may I hold him?"

Mary recognized her as the niece of old man Edward, the pitiful old gentleman who never spoke. She would talk brightly about one thing or another, while her uncle hung his head and showed no sign of hearing.

Mary and Barbara watched as the young mother lifted her little boy out of the stroller and handed him to Edward's niece.

"Oh, isn't he yummy," cooed the niece, cradling the baby tenderly in her arms and nuzzling his round cheeks with her nose.

But then there was a harsh shriek, and everyone looked up.

The cry came from old man Edward. Dorothy, the head nurse, was wheeling him from the elevator. His mouth was open, he was staring at the baby in his niece's arms and howling at the top of his lungs.

Before anyone could stop him he jerked the wheelchair out of Dorothy's control and surged forward to snatch at the baby. Words came out of his mouth. They were real words, but disconnected.

"Baby—no," gasped Edward. "She—no! No, no, no, no!"

Terrified, the young mother snatched her child back from the old man's niece, plopped him in the stroller and rushed him away to the outside door.

Left behind, the grandmother held up disappointed hands.

Edward's tangled mind seemed to have forgotten the baby. He began shouting another fragment from his old life, "Garage, park it in the garage."

His embarrassed niece hissed at him, "Shut up, Uncle Edward." She grasped the bar of his wheelchair and raced him down the hall.

But her uncle was still howling as she punched the elevator button, "Fool, you fool, you fucking, goddamned fool."

"My God, Uncle Edward." She was shouting now. "Will you *please shut up?* Jesus *God,* where's the *goddamned* elevator?"

At last the elevator doors opened, she shoved him inside, the doors closed and quiet fell.

Mary looked open-mouthed at Barbara, who merely shrugged her shoulders and muttered, "Crazy place," as though these aberrations happened all the time.

Mary kissed Barbara, said goodbye to the others and left the nursing home. She was not there to witness the anger of Edward's niece when she erupted from the elevator in a rage.

Barbara watched her march up to the reception counter and demand to see the head nurse.

Dorothy emerged from her office and looked at the woman warily. Edward's niece attacked at once.

"Dorothy, I am impoverishing myself to pay for my uncle's residence in this place. Surely relatives wishing to bring their children should call ahead."

"Yes, well—"

"Listen to me, Dorothy. I don't know whether or not you are aware that my brother is a member of the licensing board for Massachusetts nursing homes. I happen to have observed other infractions of the code. I have only to say a word to my brother and he'll—"

"What infractions? There aren't any infractions. That is an insulting suggestion."

"Nonetheless, it's true."

"All right then, I hope you'll call your brother. Tell him he's welcome to make a complete tour of inspection, any time at all, without warning. Tell him to bring along the mayor and the city council and the entire Massachusetts Board of Health. It will not be necessary to call ahead."

12

THE VIDEOCASSETTE FROM THE POCKET IN FRIEDA'S green coat began with a winter landscape of falling snow and leafless trees.

Leonard watched intently as the camera moved unsteadily through an open wood. Twiggy branches wobbled near, then flew up and out of sight.

The view opened up. It was a cemetery. Headstones and monuments were scattered among the trees—blocky shapes, an obelisk.

Whoops! Up and over. The camera gyrated wildly. Recovering its balance, it careened past a narrow tombstone with a steeple, a set of stone steps flanked by urns and a massive chunk of marble. Then, after swooping up and whirling among the treetops, it dropped with a sickening lurch to focus on a small headstone.

The image wavered and steadied, but the inscription was indecipherable. Then a light appeared at one side—a flashlight—and raked across the words. Now they could be read—

PATRICK
1990–1991

In grim concentration the camera stared at the inscription for one minute, two minutes. Leonard was forced to read it over and over—

PATRICK
1990–1991

PATRICK
1990–1991

PATRICK
1990–1991

At last the screen went black. The show was over.

To Leonard's surprise his fists were clenched. He reached forward and touched the rewind button, but the words still hung in the air—

PATRICK
1990–1991

Trying to get rid of them, he jumped out of his chair, threw open the door to the back stairs, thumped down two flights to the back door, plunged into the open air and walked around the block.

It was a big block—Sibley to Huron, Huron to Fayerweather, Fayerweather to Brattle. Swinging around the corner from Brattle onto Sibley Road, he began to run, suddenly remembering something important—that afternoon last week in the Peabody Museum and the two tall strangers who had taken such an interest in the crystals. And the next day they had joined him in the gallery.

Their name was Kelly. They were Homer and Mary Kelly from Concord. They'd be in the phone book. They were professors of something or other, but they were famous for another reason around Harvard Yard, because they had been mixed up in a number of criminal cases.

It was too much to explain on the phone. "I wonder if you people could stop by my place, next time you're in

Cambridge. It's 24 Sibley Road, the back door. I have something sort of strange to show you. I'd love to know what you people think."

"Well, fine," said Homer. "Matter of fact, we could come tonight. We both have evening classes. Is ten o'clock too late? Good, we'll be there." Then, remembering the utter impossibility of parking anywhere in the city of Cambridge, he said, "Oh, God, where do we—?"

"In the driveway. There's plenty of parking space behind the house."

"He wants to show us something strange?" said Mary, gathering her notes and pulling on her coat. "It's probably something about Escher."

"Or maybe," said Homer brightly, "he's got some really *fascinating* new crystal."

They were early, but Leonard saw their headlights as they turned into the driveway. He ran down to meet them at the back door, then led the way up to the attic.

Sitting in her kitchen in her bathrobe and slippers, Mrs. Winthrop heard the heavy footsteps and thought, *He's having a party.*

It was not a party, nor was it a discovery about M. C. Escher, nor did Leonard have a charming new crystal on display.

He wasted no time on chitchat. As soon as Homer and Mary were settled in a couple of his dingy chairs, he told them about meeting Frieda in her green coat at the gallery, and about his failure to find her afterwards.

They listened attentively, waiting for the strange thing. Leonard grimaced. "So far it's just a stupid infatuation, right?"

"Not stupid," murmured Mary.

"Very stupid," repeated Leonard. "But then I found

this."

He went to the closet and brought out the green coat. "This was hers. I found it in that fancy second-hand clothing store on Huron Av, right next to the art gallery. And there was something in the pocket, a videocassette. Wait a sec, I'll turn it on. Watch this."

It was the strange thing. In a moment Mary and Homer were caught up in the blundering progress of the camera through the cemetery and its staring concentration on a single grave—

PATRICK
1990–1991

When the screen went black they sat stunned, and then Mary whispered, "A baby. A baby's grave."

"Peculiar," muttered Homer, "the feeling of menace in that last part, where it just looks and looks."

"Exactly." Leonard was grim.

Homer jumped up, his head just missing the low rafters. "You know, I can imagine wanting to record the burial place of someone you've lost. That's not so surprising."

"Especially if it was a child," said Mary.

"Suppose the bereaved parents had a morbid desire to keep forever the memory of the grave, the flowers, the whole thing. I mean, some people are sentimental about wanting a pretty spot for a grave as though the dead body could see the view from six feet down."

"Or maybe," said Mary, "they were about to move away and didn't want to forget their baby's grave. But somehow"—she looked soberly at Leonard—"this was different."

Homer shuddered. "It was different, all right. There

was something ugly about it. No, that's not it." Thrashing around in his head, Homer pounced on the right word. "Vengeful. The whole thing was like some sort of vengeance, some kind of psychological torture."

Leonard asked an anguished question, "But why? And what does it have to do with Frieda? Why was it in her coat pocket?"

"God knows." Homer flapped his hands.

"I'll bet we could find out about the baby," said Mary.

Leonard looked doubtful. "Even without a last name?"

"Sure," said Homer. "There can't be many babies named Patrick who died in a certain year. There must be death records. Surely nobody skips off the planet without some bureaucrat licking his pencil and jotting it down."

"City Hall," said Mary wisely. "We'll try Cambridge City Hall."

"Can't do it this week," said Homer. "Five hundred god-awful term papers washing in the door like Noah's flood."

"Five hundred?" Leonard was amazed. "That's funny. I've got three or four hundred myself. You're not teaching freshmen?"

"You bet we're teaching freshmen." Homer looked at Mary, and they laughed.

Mary explained. "We like teaching freshmen. They're so wonderfully uninformed. You're writing on a blank slate, annihilating their pitiful ignorance, spreading out banquet tables of good stuff for the first time."

"Whereas," said Homer loftily, "those cozy seminars of graduate students, they're just turning over a few dry sticks."

41

"He doesn't really mean that," said Mary, picking up her coat. "Seminars are lovely. We've got some of those too."

They said goodbye and Homer began clumping down the stairs.

Leonard caught at Mary's sleeve. "I'm sorry," he said. "You people must think I'm a nut case with a really dumb obsession."

"Well, it's true," said Mary comfortably, "*I* may think you're a nut case, but don't worry about Homer. His entire life has been a parade of nutty obsessions, one right after the other. Finding a fellow nut case is what he likes best."

13

LEONARD'S INTEREST IN THE MYSTERIOUS WOMAN HE had met at the Escher exhibition was indeed foolish; in fact it was completely ridiculous, because there were a thousand things he didn't know about her.

One of the things he didn't know was that Frieda's open friendliness had not come easily. It was true that she had been a sparkling and funny little girl, but her happy childhood had been followed by an adolescence that was grimly sad. He was also unaware that their brief but intense encounter had fixed in her a resolve to move out of reach of the woman she knew as Cousin Kitty. Another unknown thing was her decision to relieve her strongly affected feelings by writing letters to a fictitious person.

Dear Random Crystallographer, began the first—

I now regard you as a long-suffering holy man with a hair shirt under your cassock, or perhaps hassock, a gaunt and saintly priest with burning eyes and wasted cheeks.

I hope you will incline your head to the curtain when I approach your confessional. I'm eager to pour my girlish feelings into your ear.

Yours, Frieda

Impossible letters like hers—and of course also Leonard's—called for an Impossible Post Office, a phantom bureaucracy already choked with Christmas letters to Santa Claus. Now in the celestial month of May it failed to deliver Frieda's ephemeral correspondence. She went on writing anyway.

Dear Random Crystallographer,

If you're not too busy, would you elope with me? Would you mind standing under the window while I climb out with my suitcase? I haven't got a ladder, so I'll have to jump, and you'll have to catch me.

Oh, yes, I know all about the force of the impact, the way it mounts up with the weight of the falling object and the distance, but I've been on a diet lately and I've packed only the filmiest of nighties. And there's a bush out there you could stagger back into. What about one day next week?

Frieda

But now, suddenly, things had changed.

She had been writing away for college catalogs, thinking seriously of going back to school. Boston University had sent her a thick volume listing their course of instruction. In the section devoted to Geological Sciences an interesting name appeared among the departmental faculty—*Leonard Underdown.* This semester Professor Underdown was teaching a course in Sedimentary Geology.

Hadn't Leonard said that he was a geologist as well as a crystallographer?

At once Frieda sat down and wrote a real letter, one that could be put into her mailbox in the downstairs entry to be picked up by a flesh-and-blood mailman and sorted inside the premises of the post office on Mount Auburn Street and delivered to a real person named Leonard Underdown in the department of Geological Sciences at Boston University.

This letter was not silly. It was discreet and modest, but it included her address and her last name.

Of course this particular address would not be good for long, because in two weeks she'd be out of here.

Moving would be easy because her shabby furniture belonged to the landlord. Frieda was glad to leave most of it behind, although she would miss the pair of mirrors that faced each other on the wall. Mrs. Larkin, her landlady, seemed to have a fixation on mirrors, because they were all over the place in the house at 87 Sibley Road, even in the back hall over the trash cans. The two in Frieda's apartment sometimes produced astonishing visions.

She certainly did not regret the loss of her green coat. Frieda had detested the green coat from the beginning because it was the gift of *Cousin* Kitty, who kept exulting in the grisly joke that their matching coats made them look like twins.

Now, thank God, she was going where Kitty would never find her.

But when Frieda brought her letter downstairs and stuck it in her letterbox, suddenly Kitty was there.

"Writing a letter to someone, dear?"

"Oh, it's just—" Frieda shook her head. "Come on upstairs, Cousin Kitty."

"Well, well, what's all this?" Kitty strode into the apartment and looked around. "Cardboard boxes? What's going on?"

"Oh, nothing," mumbled Frieda. "It's just that I've got too much stuff. I'm selling all these books to the Bryn Mawr bookstore—you know, around the corner on Huron Av." She waved at the heap of clothes on the bed. "Morgan Memorial. Sit down, Cousin Kitty."

Kitty was satisfied, but she couldn't help asking a needling question. "I wonder, dear, if you've been in touch with that man Leonard?"

"Leonard?"

"The man you met at the gallery. Remember him?"

Solemnly Frieda shook her head and said, "No, I haven't heard from him."

Well, of course she hasn't, thought Kitty. *Poor thing, she's plain as a mud fence.*

But just the same, when Kitty went downstairs she paused in the entry hall and gazed at Frieda's mailbox. Through the metal lattice she could just make out an envelope.

It was just—barely—within reach. Kitty urged it upward with her fingernails, grasped the edge and whisked it out.

When she saw the name *Leonard* on the envelope she was dumbfounded. She had thought that the man at the gallery was of no interest to her unattractive niece.

She had been wrong.

SOON ANOTHER LETTER WAS ROMPING THROUGH THE mail, the real mail, the entirely possible mail.

It was addressed to Leonard Underdown, research geologist at Boston University, student of natural surface and near-surface processes and of the erosion, transport and deposition of sediments.

The letter surprised and pleased Professor Underdown. It was a highly interesting communication from a perfect stranger who introduced herself as Professor Myrtle Greenwood of the geology faculty at Dalhousie University in New Brunswick.

This amazing woman wanted to consult him about the possible origin of the Boston Basin, because a whole new theory had occurred to her as she looked out from the tower of Mount Auburn Cemetery after attending the interment of a cousin.

She explained that she was returning to New Brunswick for a few days, but would be back in Boston next week. Might he then give her his opinion in person? He was so renowned in his field! Perhaps he could tell her whether her idea made any sense at all.

Professor Greenwood's letter ended with the suggestion that they should meet at the tower on the following Friday, if that was entirely convenient. She would be arriving in Cambridge on Thursday, when she would call to confirm the appointment.

In closing, Dr. Greenwood suggested discreetly that Professor Underdown should destroy her letter, and say nothing to anyone about this possible new theory. *People are so apt to profit unfairly from the work of others.*

THE SUICIDE WAS WITNESSED BY THE PILOT AND co-pilot of the Goodyear blimp as it floated serenely over the city of Cambridge, poising in the air like an enormous fish. Today there were no passengers in the gondola, only the two excited pilots. Instantly the pilot radioed the supervisor and passed along the horrifying news.

"My God, we saw the whole thing from a thousand feet up. There we were, right over Fresh Pond Parkway and we saw everything. This woman, she was struggling with the man, like she was trying to keep him from jumping, and then we saw the guy fall. Jesus, Jimmy, quick, call the police."

"Not the police, for Christ's sake," cried the co-pilot, grabbing the mike, "an ambulance, call an ambulance. Maybe the poor guy's not dead yet. Where? Mount Auburn Cemetery, the tower at Mount Auburn Cemetery. It just happened a minute ago. The poor guy jumped from the top of the tower, fell straight down, *kablam.*"

"There was this woman," shouted the pilot, "she just disappeared down the stairs. Now the whole thing's out of sight. Oh, shit, it'll take us five goddamned minutes to turn this thing around and get back over the fucking tower. Hang on."

IT WAS ANOTHER BEAUTIFUL DAY. MRS. WINTHROP settled herself comfortably beside Zach's stone and opened the *Boston Globe* to the obituaries. At once she gave a little cry of horror.

There on the right-hand page was a picture of Leonard, the dear boy who was her tenant! Beside the picture were terrible words.

YOUNG SCIENTIST
FALLS TO HIS DEATH.

Tears welled up in Mrs. Winthrop's eyes. She could hardly see to read. Oh, merciful God, it had happened right here. Poor Leonard had fallen from the tower *right here in Mount Auburn Cemetery*. If she stood on tiptoe the tower was visible through the trees, right up there at the top of the hill.

Only when her eyes cleared did she see that the name of the young man who had fallen from the tower was not Leonard Sheldrake. It was another Leonard entirely. And now that she looked more closely at the picture, she could see that the poor young man's face was not exactly like the face of her tenant. It had a different expression, a different sort of look.

The story was quite sensational. It was reported in detail. There had been witnesses to the suicide, observers from above, pilots of a blimp passing overhead. The pilots had seen a woman struggling with the would-be suicide, trying to keep him from making his fatal jump.

And there had also been witnesses below. A husband and wife had come running up to the dead man, and then they had tried to comfort the woman who came stumbling out of the doorway at the base of the tower.

"I tried to stop him," sobbed the woman, bending over the body in anguish. "I climbed the stairs and came out on the parapet, and there was this poor man climbing up on the railing." There was another burst of tears. She couldn't go on.

"There, there, dear," said the wife, embracing her.

"It wasn't your fault," said the husband. He gestured at the car parked on the encircling driveway. "Martha, you drive her down to the administration building and ask them to call the police. And I'll bet there's a room where she could lie down. I'll stay here and wait for the ambulance."

The police ambulance arrived, removed the body and quickly identified it as that of a young professor at Boston University. Neither his shocked colleagues nor his grieving wife could think why Leonard Underdown would wish to end his life.

The woman who had tried to prevent the apparent suicide was questioned closely, but it was clear that Eleanor Fell had no connection whatever with the deceased. Her attempt to save his life had been the generous action of a perfect stranger.

Eloise folded the newspaper, breathing a sigh of relief. It was all very sad, but thank heavens, it wasn't *her* Leonard.

The sun streaked agreeably through the trees, dappling the grass in yellow circles. At the edge of her vision Eloise was aware of a familiar dark shape. Turning, she saw the peacock stalk away in the direction of the splendid granite temple of the Lowells. She watched it eagerly, hoping that it would spread its magnificent tail.

By now she had seen it many times. It was deeply satisfying that a peacock should be here among the graves in Mount Auburn Cemetery. She had looked up the word *Peacock* in one of Zach's encyclopedias, and learned to her delight that it was a Christian symbol of everlasting life.

The peacock wandered out of sight without making the slightest effort to dazzle her with a spreading display of its glorious feathered tail.

Disappointed, she turned back to the obituary page and looked at the list of deaths. "Oh, Zach," she said aloud, "a lot of people from Cambridge crossed the bridge today. Listen to this, there are five of them. One—*Alexey, Frederick.* Two—*Buckley, Flora.* Three—*Myers, Matthew.* Four—*Schmidt, Effie Mae.*"

She read the last name on the list in perfect serenity, with no tremble in her voice at all, "Five—*Underdown, Leonard.*"

Frieda did not see the obituary for Leonard Underdown. Therefore when her letter to him received no reply, it was a harsh blow to her pride.

17

WHEN MARY AND HOMER KELLY TURNED THE PAGES of the same edition of the *Globe* it was to look at the real estate ads, not the obituary page.

"Two million five," gasped Mary. "Remember that house we walked past on Berkeley Street? The one we liked? They want two million five!"

"Well, what do you think this place on the river is worth?" grumbled Homer. "What price sublimity? Ten million in the eyes of God. I mean, compared with most of the fancy places in the real estate ads, you know, with all the usual desiderata of desirable real estate like indoor swimming pools and whirlpool baths. How about the desiderata of the sublime? That's what we've got."

Mary ran her eyes down the page. "Oh, Homer, nobody's going to pay big money for the desiderata of the sublime. They want splendid kitchens and big master bedrooms. You know the sort of thing. Unfortunately God isn't employed by a real estate firm."

"Of course he isn't, but the devil is. The devil and all his fellow fiends. Hades Estates, excellent neighborhood in the lowest pit of hell. Buy now."

"Hmmm, maybe we could afford something near Porter Square."

"Small down payment," snarled Homer. "Your immortal soul."

Mary laughed and put down the paper. "Oh, Homer, you're right, it is sickening. But, honestly, we've got to find out what our house is actually worth, I mean in crass commercial dollars and cents. I'll call somebody. More coffee?"

Glowering, Homer held out his cup. "You know what will happen to it, don't you? Somebody will buy it just for the land, and then they'll tear the house down and build a palace. Then everybody paddling on the river will curse us and we'll find ourselves in hell anyway."

Mary sat down beside Homer and changed the subject. "I wonder what that baby's grave has to do with Leonard's missing girlfriend?"

51

"Missing girlfriends," growled Homer. "Another goofy guy with a missing girlfriend. Why do we always get mixed up with missing girlfriends?"

Mary sat up, shocked. "Oh, Homer, you don't mean Julia Smith? And I suppose you call Lucia Costanza a missing girlfriend? Homer, those women might still be missing if we hadn't been there, or they'd probably be dead. Homer!"

"Well, okay, but you have to admit this female really sounds like a kook."

"Oh, she does not. And anyway, Homer, don't call women females. It's insulting."

"Why? That's what you are, aren't you? Members of the female sex."

Mary closed her eyes and set her jaw. "The question is, what does that baby's grave have to do with this mysterious woman, the one Leonard's so eager to find? I know it's idiotic, because he only met the girl once, but the poor guy is besotted, and now he can't find her. Maybe those death records in City Hall will help. At least we might find out more about the baby. When is that appointment with the clerk in City Hall?"

Gloomily Homer consulted his pocket calendar. "It's tomorrow, but I doubt it will do any good. Who knows where that woman is? Leonard's missing female is a needle in a haystack."

18

BUT AS IT TURNED OUT, LEONARD FOUND THE NEEDLE sticking straight up and shining in the sunlight in the haystack of the neighborhoods below Huron Avenue.

For two weeks he had been haunting the streets within walking distance of the gallery where he had met Frieda, looking for something, he didn't know what. A sign, a signal, a dropped handkerchief with a monogram in the corner, "F" for Frieda.

Did she live in the vicinity of Brattle Street like Mrs. Winthrop? Leonard explored the realms of light, the imposing houses on the classier reaches of Sparks, Appleton, Fayerweather, Sibley and Lakeview.

On the other side of Huron Avenue the houses diminished in grandeur. In fact Leonard could have worked out a simple mathematical formula relating the decrease in real estate value to the distance from Brattle Street.

Below Huron Av the values plummeted. But it was here on the lower part of Sibley Road that he found the needle in the haystack, the dropped handkerchief.

It was a thin rag of fluttering paper caught in a chain-link fence. The rag looked very much like—could it possibly be?

Leonard removed it carefully from the steel mesh of the fence, held it up and grinned with delight. It was a Moebius strip. At once he glanced up at the house behind the fence.

Instantly the door burst open and a woman rushed out. It was not Frieda. The woman bounded down the stairs and strode along the cement walk, her clenched fists raised, her face livid with wrath.

Leonard stood back politely as she sailed past him, and then he looked back up at the house.

It was typical of the multifamily dwellings in this part of Cambridge, a big ark with two layers of wooden porches.

A few of the other houses on the street were different.

Upmarket realtors had been at work. New owners had pulled themselves up by their bootstraps, or rather by their old firetraps. They had stripped the walls, rewired the electrical systems, replumbed the bathrooms and glorified the kitchens. The grounds had been replanted. Classy architects and landscape gardeners were doing their best to upgrade lower Sibley Road.

Many of the working-class families who had once occupied these houses had moved away. They had peered out of their windows at new neighbors from another world—young fathers rushing down the porch steps and bouncing into SUVs, young mothers with briefcases hurrying off to work, mother-substitutes pushing babies along the sidewalk in imported prams.

Leonard had noted with sardonic interest the surest sign of neighborhood gentrification. Among the heaps of newspapers on the floor of the neighborhood convenience store were many copies of the *New York Times.*

The unrehabilitated house with the chain-link fence was number 87 Sibley Road. Was it Frieda's real address, replacing the fanciful cathedral rising from the sea or the mill where the water went both up and down? Was she right here in this house, perhaps up there on the second floor behind those windows glittering with reflections of the morning sun?

Leonard opened the chain-link gate, walked past a dead plant in a concrete urn and climbed the porch steps. There was a sign beside the doorbell—

VACANCY
APPLY LARKIN

Leonard pushed the bell.

54

At once the door was hurled open by a harrassed-looking man in a bathrobe. His gray hair rose in a frowze. His eyes were wild.

"You an attorney?" he said. "Dolly's attorney?"

"An attorney? No, I just want—"

"Well, thank God. My wife, Jesus God, she just walked out on me. First thing she'll do, call her fucking attorney. Come in."

"Oh, I'm sorry."

Larkin stepped back. As Leonard walked in, there was a high soprano titter and a woman looked out from a door marked LARKIN. She grinned at Leonard, raised a glass, ducked back into the apartment and slammed the door.

Larkin closed his eyes, wiped his face with his hand and said, "God."

"I just want to ask," said Leonard quickly, "whether you have a tenant named Frieda?"

"God, I don't know," said Larkin. "What's her last name?"

Leonard tried another tack. "Might I see the empty apartment?"

Larkin heaved a deep sigh. "Second floor."

He led the way, his feet heavy on the carpeted stairs. From the basement below the stairwell rose the smell of bleach and the tumbling hum of a clothes dryer. A portly young woman with a basket of folded laundry dodged past Larkin and hurried ahead of them up the stairs.

There were two apartments on the second floor. Larkin unlocked the door on the right, and waved Leonard in, muttering an apology. "Haven't cleaned it up yet. Artist, she prolly spilled ink on the floor."

Leonard looked around at the bleak little room. "She

55

was an artist?" he said eagerly. "What was her name?"

"Hell if I know. Only here a few weeks. Paid in cash. She told me her name, I guess. I don't recall. My wife, she'd know, only—Christ."

"You mean you don't have any written record? Well, how do you know—?" Leonard was staggered. "A lease? A deposit? She gave you a check? Did she get any letters?"

"God, I don't know. She probably wasn't here long enough. Pain in the neck, her leaving so soon. Gotta rent the place all over again, advertise, big expense."

"What did she look like?"

"Well, Jesus, like I said, my wife would know. Listen, do you want the place or not?"

"May I look around?"

Larkin shrugged. "Be my guest."

Leonard took a deep breath as the landlord thumped down the stairs.

The furniture was mismatched—a bed with a clean bare mattress, a table and two chairs, a desk with a chair and a lamp, and a couple of mirrors on the wall. A kitchen counter ran along one side. A door led to a bathroom.

Looking into the bathroom, Leonard noted the traditional lattice of small octagonal white tiles on the floor. If they had been hexagonal, he told himself, they would have packed together neatly, but with octagons the pattern had to be filled out with squares.

He went back to the main room, which had windows overlooking the street. At once he saw the letter on the table, and picked it up. The name MRS. LARKIN was neatly written on the envelope. It was not sealed, and he opened it boldly. It was full of cash. And there was a note—*Next month's rent*. There was no signature.

Was this Frieda's apartment? It was probably foolish to think so. The little twisted strip of paper he had plucked from the fence might have blown here from miles away. And anybody could have made it. Cambridge was crawling with people who knew about Moebius strips. They were a commonplace intellectual toy.

But Larkin had said the former tenant was an artist who had probably spilled ink on the floor. That at least was hopeful. Frieda had said she was an artist. She made drawings, she had said, portraits of people.

There were no splashes of ink on the floor, only a few rubbishy scraps of paper from a tipped-over wastebasket. A breeze from the open window lifted the clutter of paper and slid it into the corner.

Leonard stirred the clutter with his shoe. Might there be another twisted loop of paper? A letter with her forwarding address?

No, at first he could see only advertising circulars, junk mail addressed to Occupant and a few snapshots snipped into pieces with scissors. With careful fingers he plucked out all the scraps and pocketed them. They were a puzzle to put together later.

There was also a wadded piece of heavy paper. Leonard unfolded it carefully, then nearly let it slip from his fingers. On the crumpled sheet was a sketch of a man's face. Below the face was a checkered scarf. The checks were playful. One lens of the glasses was blank, the other showed a staring eye.

Was this a try at his own face—the big nose, the glasses, the scarf?

Leonard smoothed the drawing, rolled it carefully and thrust it inside his sweater. The good things it might possibly mean were cancelled out by the bad things. If it was really a sketch of one Leonard Sheldrake, a portrait drawn from memory, she had crumpled it and thrown it away.

With a last glance around, he took two steps across the room and then stopped short. Something outrageous was happening in the mirror beside the window. It contained a thousand Leonards.

Whirlpools

*... I am working on a double spiral in woodcut ...
using a new printing technique based on a very amusing
twofold-rotation system.*

M.C. Escher

19

IT WAS LIKE THE WATER THAT MIGHT POSSIBLY BE swirling down bathtub drains in two directions above and below the equator. It was like a famous print of Escher's called *Whirlpools,* an endless double spiral of fish winding in and out of two infinitesimal centers of darkness.

How the man had delighted in infinity! Leonard knew his words by heart—*to approach infinity as purely and as closely as possible. Deep, deep infinity!*

And here it was, that miracle, enclosed in the two mirrors that faced each other on the walls of this ordinary apartment in an ordinary house on an ordinary street in the matter-of-fact city of Cambridge. A multitude of Leonards trailed back and back, shrinking and shrinking into an army of tiny Leonards receding in single file.

At once he glanced at the mirror behind him, and it was the same. Another thousand Leonards shrank and diminished behind its silvered surface. The first was a direct reflection, the second an image of Leonard's back that had flashed across the room to the other mirror. The third had made the journey twice across the room. With the speed of light the rushing Leonards fled past him.

He put out his hand as if to touch the invisible rays of light. At once all the reflected Leonards obeyed, putting out their hands in the same gesture. Impulsively he hopped and capered, laughing as all the other Leonards hopped and capered in perfect imitation. There were regiments of dancing Leonards, dimming and shrinking farther and farther back, hopping and jumping and infinitely receding into the two tiny caves that were so tightly coiled in the farthest recesses of the two facing mirrors, two remote and undiscoverable wildernesses.

"Oh, Leonard," said Mrs. Winthrop, peeking out of her kitchen door as he put a foot on the bottom step of the back stairs, "have you seen this?" She had a newspaper in her hand. "It gave me such a turn."

Leonard was half-ashamed of the way he made a practice of avoiding his landlady. He stepped down and smiled at her and took the paper. "What is it?"

"It's you," giggled Mrs. Winthrop. She pointed to the picture on the obituary page. "Doesn't it look like you? And see? His name is Leonard."

Leonard stared at the photograph of Leonard Underdown. He recognized him at once, or thought he did. This poor guy was his mirror image, the near-twin he had seen on Huron Avenue last week.

"A suicide," he said, handing the paper back. "Too bad."

Mrs. Winthrop waggled her head, her face glowing with affection. "Do you see why I was so upset?" She tapped the picture. "Doesn't he look like you?"

Leonard inspected the picture again, and shook his head. "No, he's not like me." He made a grim joke. "Look, his hair is parted on the other side." Then, aware of her gentle kindness, he said, "Mrs. Winthrop, tell me, is there anything I can do for you? Would you like me to call a roofing company?"

"A roofing company?"

"The roof, it's leaking," explained Leonard. "It would be good to repair it before next winter." He didn't explain that he was tired of emptying the bucket.

"Oh, my goodness." Mrs. Winthrop put her fragile hand to her mouth. She had been about to say that she would have to ask Zach what to do, but of course she couldn't say that. "Thank you, Leonard. I'm so grateful that you're keeping an eye on things."

He had joked about his twin's obituary, but for the rest of the day it haunted him. And that night he saw the other Leonard in a dream.

It was the double mirror again, and once again it was full of Leonards. He himself, the Leonard who was having the dream, stood at one side, watching while the others capered and threw up their arms and kicked out with their legs. Then to his surprise the two who were first in line climbed out of their frames, stepped down into the room and walked across the floor, passing each other without a glance and climbing nimbly into the opposite frame. Then with their backs to him they marched away. The other multitudinous Leonards also turned about-face. The two endless columns grew smaller and smaller and farther and farther away, until at last he could see only a squirming blackness in the farthest depths, and then that too was gone.

He woke up next morning exhausted and filled with dread. Getting out of bed and fumbling across the floor, he felt himself crouching, and tried to straighten up.

The bathroom was a nineteen-twenties modernization of the original eighteen-nineties water closet. The bathtub had claw feet and the toilet worked with a pull chain, releasing a roaring waterfall from the overhead tank. During the tumultuous weeks when Jody had butted her way into Leonard's life, she had been ecstatic. "God, they're priceless! You could sell them for real money and replace them with cheap modern stuff. Your landlady would be delighted."

The mirror over the sink showed a yellow-faced Leonard. He hated himself. His hair stuck up all over his head, pushed sideways in the wrong direction.

His watch too was on the wrong arm. He must have switched it absentmindedly last night.

But when he unstrapped the watch from his left arm, he was puzzled by the band of pale skin on his left wrist. Crazy! Why did he think he always wore his watch on the right? Obviously he didn't and never had.

Trying to wake himself up, Leonard washed his face in cold water and ran a wet comb through his hair. It was queer, the way it refused to lie flat and kept springing up under the comb.

In the end he had to part it on the other side.

20

CAMBRIDGE CITY HALL WAS A LARGE NINETEENTH-century brick fortress near Central Square, looming high above Massachusetts Avenue.

Mary and Homer walked into a vestibule lined with tributes to the veterans of various wars—*This Tablet commemorates the enlistment of the company of volunteers which was the first in the country to answer the call of President Lincoln for troops to maintain the union of the states. . . .*

"Hey," said Homer. "I didn't know that. I wonder how many of them ever came back."

The Death Records office was up a long flight of stairs. Breathing hard, Homer opened the door and they walked in. Sunlight streamed in the windows, shining on desks and file cabinets and on half a dozen clerks, all busily keeping track of the deceased citizens of Cambridge.

"May I help you?" A woman popped up in front of them, small and quick. She looked at them brightly, apparently undismayed by the mortuary nature of her job.

"We'd like to find out more about the death of an infant child in the year 1991," said Homer ponderously—he had been rehearsing the question in his head.

"The trouble is," confided Mary, leaning over the counter, "we don't know his last name. Just his first name, Patrick."

The birdlike little woman raised her eyebrows. "You don't know the last name? Well, that *does* present a problem." She stared at the ceiling and made a tent with her fingers.

"We hoped we might be permitted to examine your records for the year 1991," said Homer politely.

"After all," said Mary eagerly, "there couldn't have been very many dead babies named Patrick in the year 1991."

"No, of course not." The brisk little woman bounced away. In a moment she was back, lugging a heavy ledger. Heaving it up on the counter, she flipped the pages open. "Index book for 1860, males left column, females right, in order of date of death."

"But—," said Mary.

"Historical interest." The bright eyes snapped.

Mary was on the point of saying, "But we just want a small piece of contemporary information," then thought better of it.

Homer of course did not complain at all. Recognizing

a barmy fellow enthusiast, he understood at once that history came first and information second.

"Well, how fascinating," he said warmly, "Ms.—"

"Puckett. Amelia Puckett."

"Ms. Puckett, would you explain it to us, the way records were kept at that time?"

"Oh, yes, Ms. Puckett," said Mary, nodding and grinning from ear to ear, "please do."

Amelia Puckett beamed and ran her finger down the page. "All handwritten, of course. Note that many of these people were immigrants. In the column for *Place of Origin,* you can see that many were born in another country. Look, see here? *Ireland, Ireland, Italy, Ireland.*"

"Hey," said Homer, "my grandparents must be in here somewhere. Potato-famine Irish. They met on the boat."

Mary propped her elbows on the counter and watched patiently while Amelia Puckett and Homer pored excitedly over the 1860 book, and then through an even heavier one for the year 1863.

"Battle of Gettysburg," murmured Ms. Puckett reverently, tapping the ledger. "That's why there are so many." Mary and Homer watched her finger run gravely down the listings of dead young men. This, then, was what had happened to the company of gallant volunteers on the memorial tablet downstairs.

Bang! Enough of that! Amelia Puckett slapped the book shut and dragged it away. When she came waltzing back, she was carrying the computerized volume for the year 1991.

"It's all yours," she said cheerily, thumping it down on the counter and bouncing away.

They huddled over it. "It's so thick," whispered

66

Mary. "Look how many Cambridge people died in the year 1991. Golly."

"Don't forget," muttered Homer, running his finger down the first page, "this is a big city with a hundred-thousand people, that's what Leonard tells me." Homer's finger stopped near the bottom of the page. "Hey, here's somebody named Patrick. *Patrick Michael Summers.* Mmmm, let's see how old he was when he died."

Mary craned her neck. "Eighty-one, Homer. Wrong Patrick. Who's next?"

Slowly they turned the pages, pausing at Patrick after Patrick. Homer was amused. "Good Irishmen all," he said, turning another page, "immigrants from County Cork and County Galway and County Limerick."

"Oh, Homer, these people weren't immigrants. Look, they were born here."

"Well, the children of immigrants then, or the grandchildren. Even so, they remembered Patrick, the saint who drove the snakes out of Ireland."

Halfway through the ledger they found a Patrick who had been born in 1990, obviously an infant at the time of his death in 1991. His name was Patrick O. Fell.

"Fell," said Homer, disappointed. "Not Finnegan? Flannery, McDuffy?"

"Oh, Ms. Puckett?" called Mary. "We think we've found him."

Amelia Puckett trotted over and looked at the entry for Patrick Fell. "How sad," she said. "Infant deaths are always so sad."

Swiftly she whirled around and scurried across the room. Mary and Homer watched as she ransacked a file cabinet, whisked out documents and plunged into another drawer for more.

In a moment she was back with a handful of papers. *Slap, slap,* they were spread out on the counter.

Mary scribbled it all down—

> Patrick O. Fell
> Date of birth, March 19, 1990
> Date of death, May 29, 1991
> Cause of death, automobile accident
> Place of burial, Mount Auburn Cemetery

"Mount Auburn," said Homer. "But, my God, it's so huge. How will we ever—?"

"Records," interrupted the mortuary archivist joyfully. "Mount Auburn keeps records of all their burials. Meticulous, absolutely meticulous. And it's such a beautiful garden. Truly inspiring. You'll see."

They thanked her and she tripped away, beaming.

"I love enthusiasts," murmured Homer.

Mary slung the strap of her bag over her shoulder. But before turning away she glanced at another ledger lying open on the counter.

"Look, Homer," she whispered, "it's for this year."

"So it is," said Homer. "Right up to the minute."

He glanced at the latest recorded death in the city of Cambridge, the suicide of someone named Leonard Underdown. He had been only thirty-six years old.

Sad. It was another sad case

21

LEONARD AND HOMER MET AT THE MONUMENTAL entrance to Mount Auburn Cemetery. "I've seen this all my life," said Homer, "but I've never been inside."

The entrance was a monumental Egyptian gate. It spoke of ancient tombs along the Nile and colossal pharaohs rising out of the desert.

"Listen, Homer," whispered Leonard.

But Homer said, "This way." He strode through the gate and turned left in the direction of the administration building, a one-story stone structure in a nest of pretty plantings.

Leonard began to follow, then stopped to stare anxiously at the landscape of tall trees and grass and gravestones. With a pang, he remembered that ninety-thousand people were buried in this place. Mount Auburn was a city of the dead.

Homer looked back, and Leonard hurried to catch up. "Where's Mary?" he said uneasily. "I thought she was coming."

"Visiting a friend. Old friend in a nursing home."

"Listen, Homer, I've found her apartment."

"What?" Home had forgotten the original purpose of their investigation. "Whose apartment?"

"Frieda's. At least I think it was hers."

Homer stopped short and stared at him. "You mean you've found her? The woman you've been looking for?"

"No, unfortunately I haven't. She's moved away."

"Oh, Christ. Look, here we are."

The sign said OFFICE. Homer led the way into a large room bright with sunshine from a skylight overhead. A woman with grey hair and pink cheeks stood up from a desk and asked politely what she could do to help.

"We're—uh—looking for someone's grave," began Homer, expecting a succession of bureaucratic delays, forms to fill out, explanations of intent. "A child's grave. His name was Patrick Fell."

And then to his surprise the receptionist at Mount Auburn turned out to be as helpful as the vivacious little woman at City Hall.

"Of course." Instead of bustling away to heave giant ledgers off a distant shelf, the pink-cheeked woman pulled open a drawer on her side of the counter. "We have that information right here."

"Well, good," said Homer happily, leaning over to look.

Her fingers twiddled in the drawer. "We call this the roll call of the dead."

"Tarantara," said Homer cheerfully, getting in the spirit of the thing. Leonard flinched.

"There's a card for every burial. Let—me—see. Yes, here it is, the Deceased Card for Patrick Fell." She plucked out a small yellow card and read it aloud. "Patrick Fell, Narcissus Path. Date of interment June 7, 1991. Order signed by Edward Fell, father. Undertaker, Hornby and Son, Cambridge."

She showed them the card. "It's yellow, you see, not white. That means it was a regular burial, not a cremation."

"Bingo," said Homer, amazed. He looked triumphantly at Leonard, who seemed stupefied. Then Homer spread his hands in a gesture of bewilderment. "But where's Narcissus Path? How will we ever find

70

it?"

Pink-cheeks smiled. "Nothing to it." She reached across the counter to a display of pamphlets, took out a map of the cemetery and spread it on the counter.

"This is where you are right now," she said, pointing, "right down here at the entrance." Her finger traced a looping line along green and white avenues and dotted paths. It stopped and tapped at a spot. "Here's Narcissus Path, near Auburn Lake."

"Oh, thank you, that's great." Homer fumbled in his pants pocket. "How much is the map?"

"Take it," she said. "The next one will be a quarter."

"Excuse me," said someone, pushing forward. "I'd like to speak to the genealogist about my distinguished family." He was frowning. "I think I spoke to you before."

"Oh, yes, I remember," said the receptionist. Her pink cheeks became pinker. "Do you have an appointment?"

The descendant of the distinguished family was a short tubby man in a grey suit. "An appointment? No, I do not have an appointment. Isn't the genealogist a regular employee? Isn't it her job to receive inquiries?"

Homer grinned at Leonard and nodded his thanks to the kindly receptionist, who was under siege, and they walked out of the building.

"Hey, Leonard," he said, "have you got a bunch of distinguished ancestors?"

"Ellis Island," said Leonard. "Frightened immigrants from Uzbekistan. Babushkas, babies, bags and bundles."

"Well, I told you about mine, Micks escaping the potato famine. Mary's are another story. Noble Concord farmers."

"Well, the hell with genealogy anyway," said Leonard. Gloomily he followed Homer to the parking lot, thinking about the roll call of the dead, picturing a beefy sergeant at arms barking out the names of those on the brink of death—

"Jones?"

"Here!"

"Smith?"

"Here!"

"Sheldrake?"

"Here!"

"Okay, you knuckleheads, fall in!"

And then, one by one, they would keel over into the trench—all the terminal cases, the battle fatalities with their bleeding wounds, the wheezing tuberculars, the mangled accident victims, and of course the occasional dismal suicide.

22

MRS. WINTHROP HAD SET OUT FOR MOUNT AUBURN that morning a full half hour after Leonard, but she was comfortably settled in her favorite neighborhood long before Leonard and Homer found their way to Narcissus Path, because they kept getting lost.

"We must have made a wrong turn back there," mumbled Leonard. "This isn't Beech Avenue, it's Cypress."

"Wow, talk about Egypt, look at the sphinx."

The sphinx was a Civil War memorial celebrating the Emancipation Proclamation and the preservation of the Union. They admired it respectfully, and Homer told Leonard about the names of the dead for the year 1863 in the ledger at City Hall.

Again they consulted the map. "Left," said Homer, "we go left on Cedar."

Cedar led to Walnut, which strangely lost itself in Poplar, which disappeared into Larch. Here there was a dispute. Homer wanted to reverse direction and go right on Willow.

"No, no," whispered Leonard, "left on Oak."

They compromised by getting lost among pretty paths named for flowers—Rhodora, Rosemary, Jasmine.

In the meantime Mrs. Winthrop had left her post beside her husband's grave because something exciting was happening on Beech Avenue. Through the trees she could see a funeral procession. The first vehicle was full of flowers, and then came the long grey hearse. The two dignified automobiles were moving very slowly, followed by a parade of friends and relatives in ordinary cars.

She would watch! Mrs. Winthrop stood up and stumbled along Willow Avenue. Fortunately the interment was nearby, and she was able to catch up. Respectfully she stood behind an obelisk, not wanting to interfere.

The procedure was familiar. The casket was taken from the hearse and placed on a contraption that would lower it into the ground, and then it was covered with flowers.

So pretty! The deceased's loved ones had spared no expense. There were lilies and delphiniums, carnations and roses, daisies and snapdragons.

Of course, observed Eloise a little snobbishly, there were not as many for this person as there had been for Zachariah. For *his* interment there had been far too many flowers for the lid of the casket. The rest had been heaped around it like a garden. And there had been flowery tributes from colleagues all over the world.

But after all, Eloise reminded herself smugly,

Zachariah Winthrop had been *Zachariah Winthrop.* Who, she wondered, was being honored with this modest display today?

She watched as the clergyman straightened his stole and opened his book. The gathering moved closer. One young woman was sobbing quietly. *The bereaved wife,* thought Eloise with rapt attention. *Or perhaps the grieving daughter.*

But when the clergyman began to speak, she understood at once. This was the interment of the poor young man who had killed himself, the one whose picture in the paper had looked so much like her dear tenant. The name the clergyman pronounced was *Leonard Underdown.*

And, good heavens—from Mrs. Winthrop's courteous distance behind the obelisk, she recognized a familiar person. It was the mother of the dead baby, the handsome woman who was always so faithful to the resting place of dear little Patrick. She must be a relative of the Underdowns. How amazing!

When the clergyman closed his book and the mourning friends and relatives began drifting away, moving toward their cars, Eloise saw with sympathy that the dead baby's mother was walking with the bereaved wife. She had her right arm tucked into the wife's arm and with her gloved left hand she patted the wife's limp wrist.

"Oh, you were so good," moaned Margaret Underdown, leaning on her new friend. "Father and I are so grateful. You tried to save my husband." There was a fresh burst of tears. "Thank you, oh, thank you."

"Tell me, dear"—there was an uneasy note in the new friend's voice—"was your husband interested in art at all?"

"Art?"

"Yes. You know, gallery openings, prints, that sort of thing."

"Oh, no, never. Lennie wasn't like that, not a bit." Margaret Underdown seemed a little insulted. Proudly she said, "A man's man, that was my Lennie."

Mrs. Winthrop was too far away to hear this exchange. From behind the obelisk she guessed that Patrick's mother was the older sister of the poor little wife. *Having endured one unbearable tragedy, she is wise in the ways of grief. She can comfort poor Mrs. Underdown.*

On the way back to Willow Avenue, Mrs. Winthrop saw the peacock again, ducking under a dogwood tree to nibble at a daffodil. She spoke to it severely. "Shame on you, peacock! Why didn't you appear at the interment and spread your tail as a symbol of everlasting life?"

But it hadn't. Eloise walked slowly back to Zachariah, remembering that there was something she had meant to ask him. Nestling on her blanket as close to his tall stone as she dared—respecting the rule that the monuments were not to be touched—she asked Zach her question about the house of which he had once been lord and master. There seemed to be a leak in the roof. What should she do?

Wisely he advised her to wait. Perhaps the problem would go away by itself.

"Oh, yes," breathed Eloise, getting to her feet and folding her blanket. "And, oh, Zach, the weatherman predicts nothing but sunshine all next week."

23

PATRICK'S EXHAUSTED MOTHER MADE HER WAY TO her child's grave and stretched out beside it, pillowing her right cheek on the soft green moss, remembering what had been done to her. The chubby face of her lost child never left her consciousness. The passage of time had not blurred the memory of his cunning face, his bright eyes and yellow curls.

And he had been so bright, so quick. Oh, yes, he had been a handful—how he had screamed when he didn't get his way! But how could she have refused such a darling, such a clever little boy, the precious child for whom she had waited so long, for whom she had suffered one miscarriage after another and been crushed by the keenest disappointment so many, many times? Until at last, thank God, little Patrick had been born into the world alive and well. He had laughed as soon as he saw the light! He had been talking in sentences at eleven months and at thirteen months he had been reading his little books.

But then that pitiful little hobgoblin had murdered him. She had destroyed the precious child who might have been the hope of the world.

Had they arrested her, had they tried her for murder and imprisoned her for the rest of her life? They had not. And then Edward, foolish, sentimental Edward, had insisted on taking her in.

It was because the brat had lost her parents the next day. Edward's sister and brother-in-law had been killed the very next day in a spectacular aircraft disaster. The controversial investigation had been in the news for months. Three-hundred-and-sixty-two people had perished in a flaming plunge into the Atlantic.

"The poor kid," Edward had said. "She's so bereft. Why can't she take Patrick's place?"

As if a gawky teenage girl in the ghastliest stages of adolescence could ever take the place of her angel child! But then it had occurred to her that she could punish the girl in a thousand little ways, and she had agreed.

And vengeance was what she wanted. She had made a heartfelt vow—*the little bitch would never have a child of her own.*

Oh, but it was cold, it was suddenly so cold. Wrenching herself up from her mossy bed, Patrick's mother struggled to her feet. For a moment she scrabbled in her pocketbook, then hurried away down the hill, limping and staggering at first, then walking easily along Linden Path.

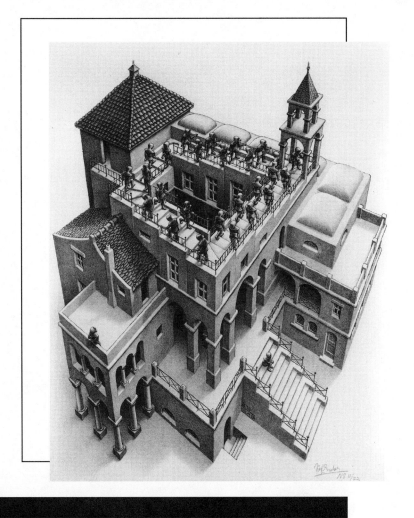

Ascending and Desending

That staircase is a rather sad, pessimistic subject, as well as being very profound and absurd . . . Yes, yes, we climb up and up, we imagine we are ascending . . .and where does it get us? . . .How absurd it all is . . .

M.C.Escher

24

THE BABY'S GRAVE, WHEN THEY FOUND IT AT LAST, was one of a huddle of monuments enclosed within a granite curb. In the middle of the plot an angel stood on tiptoe above a tall stone inscribed with the word fell.

"Here he is," said Homer. "Look, Patrick Fell in person."

They stood at the back of the plot looking down at the familiar little headstone—

PATRICK
1990–1991

There was a sound of purring engines. Beyond the trees a funeral procession moved slowly down Beech Avenue.

Homer shook his head in disapproval. "Why don't they throw people's ashes to the four winds?" He waved his hand at a row of gravestones marking the resting places of various members of the Story family. "Outworn tribal custom, cluttering up the landscape with a bunch of bones. All those people had their turn in the sun. Why clutter up the earth under our feet?"

Leonard said nothing. Mesmerized, he watched the last car disappear in the direction of the great Egyptian gate.

The hum of engines faded. The procession was gone. But then, to Leonard's amazement, another took its place.

This time it wasn't cars, it was people. They were

approaching. A black-veiled woman tramped sternly in the lead, followed by four men carrying on their shoulders a small casket. The men too were all in black. Their heads were bowed, they made no sound.

"Look," whispered Leonard, touching Homer's arm.

"Ouch," said Homer, tripping over something. He had been walking around Patrick's little headstone, hoping to find an inscription on the back. Staggering, he looked down. "Hey, there's something on the ground back here in this bush."

Leonard was not listening. The walking procession had passed so close to him that the woman's veil floated out and brushed his sleeve. Now she was climbing the steep slope behind the family plot, moving upward between the row of Storys and a steepled monument marking the grave of Nathan Appleton.

The pallbearers were climbing too, shouldering their burden. The procession mounted the steep little hill, climbing easily and silently, and disappeared among the trees.

"It's a metal box," said Homer. He stooped and picked it up. "Christ, there's a letter inside."

Leonard blinked. "A letter?"

They sat together on the granite curb and looked at the envelope. It was addressed to *Patrick*.

Homer slipped out the letter, but Leonard was distracted. The strange little procession was coming back, descending the hill as easily as they had climbed it only a moment before. Had they lost their way?

Homer read the letter aloud—

Darling boy,
It's your twelfth birthday! I'm so proud of you! To

*be doing so well in school, and to be a hero on the
soccer field as well! Your grandfather would be
proud of you too! He'd say you're a chip off the old
block. You're perpetuating the family name with
distinction!*

Your loving Mother

Homer looked at Leonard and said, "Sick, really
sick."

"Right," said Leonard.

Homer folded the letter and put it back in the
envelope. "Listen, Leonard, I've got the rest of the
afternoon free. How about we take the Red Line and the
Green Line to the Boston Public Library? Nothing to it.
Then we could look up the kid's obituary. How about
it? We might learn something useful."

"Well, okay," mumbled Leonard, but his attention
was wandering. The soundless parade of mourners had
come back. The veiled woman was leading her little
band up the hill for the second time.

They were ascending and descending and ascending
again, going around and around without end, like the
little men on Escher's impossible staircase.

25

THE NOON HOUR WAS THE BEST TIME TO BE ALONE
with Barbara in the Aberdeen Street Nursing Home,
because her roommate would not be there. Jenny always
took her meals in the dining room.

Jenny was a whimsical old woman, amusing,

affectionate and troublesome because she kept pushing open the outside door and setting off the alarm. Whenever Mary came to see Barbara, Jenny hugged her and patted her face and said, "You don't like me, do you?" And then Mary would hug her back and say, "Yes, I do," because it was true.

But today Mary had been caught in a faculty meeting until midafternoon. In the nursing home she found Barbara's wheelchair parked among the rest across from the nurses' station.

Mary had brought along her book of Escher prints.

"Oh, yes," said Barbara, turning the pages. "I remember this one, the tower of Babel."

Mary pointed to the little workmen at the top of the tower, gesturing and waving their arms. "Did you read what he said about it? They can't build it any higher because they're all talking different kinds of babble. They can't understand each other any more."

At once they both thought of the senile residents of the nursing home, men and women whose speech had been reduced to meaningless confusion.

Mary glanced at Jenny and Wilma. The two old ladies were sitting quietly in their wheelchairs gazing into space. They had been cast away, each on her own desert island, no ship on the horizon, no white sail, no band of sailors running up the beach to carry them back to active life.

Barbara turned the page.

As usual a few people were visiting their relatives. Shirley had a visitor, and so did Henry. Fortunately none of the visitors had brought babies. There were no distressing scenes. At least not until Mary was about to leave.

Then, as she told Homer afterwards, all hell broke

loose.

There was a terrible noise, a shriek followed by a racket of thumping crashes like elephants falling downstairs.

It was not elephants, it was poor old Edward. He burst headlong through the door at the bottom of the stairs, his legs entangled in his wheelchair as it rattled across the floor on its side, bouncing and scraping, shoving him forward, smashing his head against the wall.

Mary jumped up. A chambermaid dropped her vacuum cleaner. Dorothy ran around the counter.

The crashing had stopped but not the noise. Edward's niece came clattering down the stairs. Screaming, she stumbled across the floor, bent over her uncle and shrieked, "He's dead, isn't he? He's dead!"

"What happened?" cried Dorothy, dropping to her knees. "What on earth happened?"

"I had my back turned," gasped Edward's niece. "Just for a second, because I was pushing the elevator button. Oh, my God." She stared at her uncle's open mouth and staring eyes. "Is he dead?"

Dorothy sat back on her knees. Her face was grim. "You mean he got through that heavy door to the stairway all by himself?"

"He must have," whimpered the niece. "When I turned around, he was through the door and heading for the stairs. I couldn't get to him in time." She covered her face with her hands. "I couldn't stop him." Her shoulders shook with sobs. "I just couldn't stop him."

Dorothy jumped to her feet and ran to call the resident doctor. The chambermaid backed away. The old women lined up along the wall were waving their arms and crying. Barbara sat with bowed head. Mary

85

took her hand.

Edward's niece was still sniffling and talking to herself, but above her boohooing they could hear the urgency in Dorothy's voice as she spoke into the phone. "No, not that Edward, Doctor Quince. You remember our Edward, here in Unit Three, the old man who—yes, that's the one. Edward Fell."

Mary kissed Barbara and said goodbye, then joined the other departing visitors, who were all in a state of shock. Together they walked out of the Aberdeen Street Nursing Home, leaving it to recover from the latest of its endless sorrows.

26

IT WAS EASY ENOUGH TO FIND THE OBITUARY FOR Patrick Fell. Easy, that is, for Leonard, who was an old pro with electronic equipment. Homer was all thumbs. Leonard sat at a terminal in the spacious grandeur of Philip Johnson's enormous addition to the Boston Public Library, trying to call up the index to the *Boston Globe* for the year 1991.

"My God," said Homer, looking around. "There used to be a room full of wooden file cabinets in this library, row upon row. Dozens of them. Hundreds of file drawers. Millions and billions of file cards. Oh, well, what the hell, it's like this at Harvard too. That marvelous old catalog room in Widener, remember? With its high ceiling and marble columns and all those old wooden file cabinets?"

"No," said Leonard. "I don't remember."

He didn't remember? Leonard was too young to

remember? At once Homer was aware of his own superannuation. Involuntarily he put up one arm to ward off the looming shove of a future that was cramming everything into the funnel of the past, thrusting into a narrow hole all the years when he had been one of the lords of creation—well, not exactly one of the tiptop lords, but maybe one of the lesser ones—well, no, not even a lesser lord but at least a hanger-on—in that happy time when the entire world had not been choked with plump young faces, healthy and pink, with clever bright eyes that knew him not.

Homer stared angrily at the shifting images on the monitor and shrugged. Well, after all, how could those kids possibly know an old feller named Homer Kelly? He could feel himself becoming invisible. Before long he would disappear completely. "Sad," he said, shaking his head, profoundly depressed. His self-esteem, that fragile urn in the front hall of his being, was beginning to crack.

"Okay, here we are," said Leonard, hunched over the keyboard. "Look at this."

Pulling himself together, Homer leaned over Leonard's shoulder. The obituary was brief—

PATRICK O. FELL
ACCIDENT VICTIM

Patrick Fell, 18 months old, was killed by a hit-and-run driver Monday evening after wandering into the street from an open door. Reportedly, the baby had been left alone by his cousin, who was babysitting.

Patrick was the only child of Mr. and Mrs. Edward Fell of Cambridge. The funeral will be private.

Leonard printed it out, Homer pulled up a chair and they looked at it together.

"Hmmmm," said Homer, "it reminds me of that grisly videocassette."

Leonard nodded solemnly, and whispered, "It's another accusation—*left alone by his cousin.* You don't see that kind of thing in obituaries usually, do you? I mean, isn't it mostly just the bare facts?"

"And *only child of*—it underscores the accusation. I feel sorry for the babysitter. The poor kid was probably scarred for life."

Together they took the Green Line back to Park Street and then the Red Line to Harvard Square. During the tiresome double journey, Leonard sat hunched and silent, saying little in response to Homer's impulsive bursts of conversation. When the train stopped at Harvard Square, they said goodbye and Homer watched Leonard shuffle out of the car onto the platform. Before the doors closed Homer jumped up and shouted, "Hey, Leonard, are you all right?"

Leonard looked back in surprise and nodded, and Homer had to jump back in a hurry to avoid the closing slap of the doors.

Slowly climbing the stairs to Church Street, clinging to the railing, Leonard thought about little Patrick Fell, who was coiled in the dark depths of the spiral, the remotest cave in the mirror. Surely the child was the key to everything.

27

WHEN HOMER ROLLED HIS CAR CAREFULLY DOWN THE steep descent beside the river, Mary was there ahead of him, just back from the harrowing scene in the nursing home. Homer waited behind the wheel while she swooped her car around, zoomed into reverse, and parked at the edge of the woods. Then Homer swooped around too and parked beside her.

They popped out simultaneously. Each was full of news. Their revelations meshed.

They were both exhausted. "I need this," said Homer, snatching a bottle of wine from the pantry. They sat down with brimming glasses, and Mary gaped at Homer's printout of the 1991 obituary for little Patrick Fell.

"Oh, my God, Homer, the father's name was Edward Fell?" She batted the printout and looked up in agitation. "Could he possibly be the same Edward Fell?"

"What do you mean, the same Edward Fell?"

"The one in Barbara's nursing home. Remember, I told you about that senile old man and his niece? Homer, I'll bet it's the same Edward Fell. He made that awful scene when somebody brought in a baby, I told you about that, remember? Well, today his wheelchair fell down the stairs and he was killed. I saw it. I was there."

Homer couldn't believe it. "Patrick's father? You mean he was in the same nursing home with Barbara? You saw *what?*"

"Oh, it was god-awful. Homer, I think his niece pushed the wheelchair down the stairs. I think she killed

89

him on purpose."

"Oh, come on."

"No, really. It's what she said. She claimed he got away from her when she was taking him to the elevator on the second floor. But Dorothy—she's the head nurse—she didn't see how he could have opened the heavy door by himself. There's a door between the elevator and the stairs. Edward would have had to pull it inward first, then hold it open while he maneuvered the wheelchair through—pretty hard for a weak old man."

"So she might have pushed him down the stairs? His niece, you say? She was the one who pushed him?"

It dawned on them both simultaneously. "The cousin," said Mary, "she must be the cousin."

"Right." Homer slapped the table. "Edward Fell's niece was Patrick Fell's cousin. She must be the babysitter who left him alone."

"And now maybe she's killed again," said Mary. "And maybe it was on purpose this time, not an accident. Maybe she was tired of carrying around the guilt for the death of her baby cousin, twelve years ago, and now she was alarmed by the way the baby's senile old father was blabbing about it, making scenes about babies. I told you about that, Homer, the way he yelled at her about babies. Maybe she wasn't just embarrassed, maybe she was afraid the whole miserable story would come out again."

"Aren't you making a good many leaps in the dark?" said Homer, who had been known to make a few crazy leaps in the dark himself. "If the man called Edward Fell in the nursing home was old and senile, how could he have been the father of a baby only twelve years ago?"

"Oh, I know, I said he was old and senile, but it

90

depends on what you call old. Barbara knows the histories of some of the people in the nursing home— Jenny and Bob, Wilma and Shirley. She told me Edward was sixty-eight. So twelve years ago he would have been only fifty-six. That's not too old to become the father of a baby, as long as his wife was still capable of conceiving. Barbara said his dementia was the result of a stroke in his middle sixties. And, listen, Homer, there's something else." Mary jumped up, knocking over her empty wine glass. "Oh, hell, wait a minute."

Homer got down on his knees and helped her pick up the pieces. "You know, Mary dear, you're showing your age. Nobody says oh hell any more. Ask the kids in your classes. You know what they say."

"Oh, I know perfectly well what they say." A shard of glass stabbed Mary's thumb. "They say shit. Oh, Homer, I can't say shit. To me oh hell is perfectly adequate. It means total frustration and fury and despair. Ouch." She sucked her thumb.

"Well, I'm rather fond of it myself," said Homer. "Hold still. I'll get the antiseptic." He disappeared into the bathroom and came back. "Damn is nice too in its adorable gentle way." He sprayed Mary's thumb and struggled with a Band Aid. "And sometimes, of course, goddamn it to hell has a sweetly old-fashioned ring."

Mary took another glass out of the kitchen cupboard. "More wine, Homer? What was I going to say? Something about—oh, I know. What does all this have to do with the woman named Frieda? Why on earth did she have that strange video in her coat pocket?"

"Damned if I know," said Homer. "And we don't even know for sure that the coat was hers." He turned scornful. "Love at first sight! The man's off his rocker."

"It's a lovely thought just the same," said Mary

wistfully.

"What is?" growled Homer. "You mean love at first sight?"

"Of course I mean love at first sight. But it's totally irrational, of course. Completely and utterly irrational." Mary sighed, feeling a little tipsy. "Too bad."

28

READING THE DEATH NOTICES IN THE *GLOBE* A WEEK later, Mrs. Winthrop ran her eyes swiftly down a list that included the name of Edward Fell. The name meant nothing to her until the day of his interment.

Then, peering through the trees once again, she saw a parade of cars on Beech Avenue. This time they were not moving up the hill, they were slowing down and stopping.

She watched eagerly as a casket was trundled among the trees. *Why, good gracious, they were coming this way.* Leaning over the edge of the slope above Narcissus Path, Eloise saw to her astonishment that flowers had been heaped near Patrick's little grave. It must be a family burial for someone related to the dear little boy.

She scrambled to her feet and felt her way cautiously down the grassy hill, teetering and clutching at twigs. At the foot of the slope she scurried across the grass and stood behind the tall monument marking the last resting place of Supreme Court Justice Joseph Story, one of the most distinguished of Zach's neighbors.

Oh, yes, it was surely a family interment, because here again among the mourners was the baby's mother, the good-looking woman who cared for Patrick's little grave so tenderly. Eloise was shocked to see that only a few other people had come to honor the deceased. And the display of flowers was really rather pitiful.

She watched as Patrick's mother dabbed at her face with a handkerchief. It was obvious that she was not really crying. It was just a polite show of grief, a courtesy to the dear departed, whose name—Mrs. Winthrop could just catch the words of the minister's kindly homily—was Edward Fell.

She vowed to look again at the most recent obituary pages. Probably Mr. Fell had been terribly old and ill, and therefore his crossing of the bridge between life and death could be called a blessing.

As her own would be. To cross the bridge and be with Zach for all eternity! Eloise had already written the instructions for her burial. Her inscription would be added to his stone just below the ringing list of his honors and accomplishments—

And his wife
ELOISE CREECH WINTHROP
1921—

29

LEONARD DID NOT WITNESS THE INTERMENT OF Edward Fell. When he crept up the hill next day to take another look at Patrick's grave, he was merely checking the letterbox. Had any more messages been mailed to the Great Post Office in the sky? It struck him that communications addressed to a dead baby were no more absurd than his own latest letter to—

Ms. Frieda X
The House of Stairs
If undeliverable at this address please forward to —
Another World
or try—
The Belvedere

But as he trudged up Beech Avenue Leonard forgot about his mission and made a detour on Linden Path to pay his respects to the octahedron.

So far in Leonard's explorations of the cemetery he had found a magnificent polished sphere and a tall flat triangle. Somewhere, he knew, there was a cube balanced on one corner, as though to symbolize the transcendance of the spirit, its freedom from the physical laws of gravitation and bodily decay. But the octahedron was the best.

It wasn't really an octahedron, it was an insanely multifaceted polyhedron of polished hornblende gabbro dedicated to various members of the Smith family. Behind it, as though the octahedron had laid an egg, was a child's grave in the shape of a tiny pyramid, a sad but witty afterthought.

Was the bereaved person who had designed this fantastic monument a crystallographer? One like himself, for instance? If he, Leonard, were to invent an elaborate geometrical tombstone for himself, what shape would it be? A tetrahexahedron? A pentagon-trioctahedron? Or a ditetragonal dipyramid like the crystals of rutile?

Shivering, he turned on his heel and tried to find his way back to Beech Avenue, but the paved road failed to

94

show itself. Instead he was treading a nameless little lane, and here beside the path was the tomb of Henry Wadsworth Longfellow. What was *he* doing here? Poets shouldn't jump around in this bewildering way long after they were dead and gone.

Oh, God, he was lost. The place was a labyrinth. And, Christ, here was the octahedron again. He was going around in a circle. Or maybe on a Moebius strip. Maybe he was trapped in a loop with a single repeating surface.

Therefore Leonard was not surprised when the melancholy procession with the miniature casket appeared again, marching silently toward him. He slumped against a tree while it floated by. Would it reappear? Yes, here they were again, ascending and descending like the people on Escher's miraculous staircase.

This time the grim lady at the head of the parade glanced at him as she passed by. Through her veil he could just make out a piercing stare.

Leonard pulled himself to his feet and shambled after the last of the crouching figures with the little casket. Maybe *they* knew where the hell they were going. *He* certainly didn't.

Yes, here was Narcissus Path, just where it ought to be, and beside it was the burial plot devoted to little Patrick and the family Fell. The procession climbed noiselessly away, mounting the sharp ascent to Willow Avenue, but Leonard stayed behind, astonished to see a heap of withered flowers next to Patrick's little headstone.

It was a new grave. How strange! It had never occurred to Leonard that another Fell might join the rest. He had not been aware that any part of this piece of mortuary real estate was unoccupied. Who was the new resident?

He would ask at the administration building, where all the sepulchral information would be entered neatly on a little card. But first—warily Leonard opened the dismal mailbox behind Patrick's grave to see if there were any more letters from the madwoman to her dead son.

Yes, another envelope lay in the box. Leonard stared at the limp pale square, not wanting to read it, wishing it would disappear. Nervously he thrust his fingers into his hair, trying to push it sideways and smooth it down. Instead it bounced up like so many springs and flopped back in the wrong direction.

With reluctant fingers he opened the envelope. The new letter was crazier than the last—

Patrick dear,

I know how eager you are to talk to me, to tell me everything.

I'm trying, dear heart, I'm doing my best. But that Madame Ronda was no good at all. She told me to find other interests, as if there could be any other interest in my life but reaching you at last!

Your loving Mother

At the counter in the Administration Building Leonard was greeted politely by the pink-cheeked woman who had helped them before. This time she introduced herself. Her name was Lydia Thompson, and she was the archivist for Mount Auburn. She knew its entire history. She was acquainted with the lives and genealogies of all its most famous occupants, from Edward Everett to Mary Baker Eddy and Buckminster

96

Fuller.

Leonard asked his question bluntly, "Can you tell me who was buried recently on Narcissus Path?" For a moment Mrs. Thompson looked blank, and he added, "Or is it none of my business?"

She smiled and said, "Of course I can tell you. Just a moment." She turned to her desk and consulted a calendar. "It was a sixty-eight-year-old gentleman. His name was Edward Fell."

"I see." Leonard thought a minute. Mrs. Thompson looked at him expectantly. "Can you tell me in what way he's related to the other people buried there?"

"You could ask his niece Eleanor Fell. She was the one who handled it. No, I'm wrong." Leonard was surprised to see the plump kindly face turn a little sour. "I should have said, Eleanor *Oliphant* Fell. Our genealogist has been trying to help her with possible regal connections in her ancestry." Mrs. Thompson's tone was carefully formal, but there was a slight mocking emphasis on the word *regal.*

He asked another intrusive question, not sure how far his inquisitiveness could go. "Tell me, how do you know whether there's room underground for another burial? Do you have any sort of—what do you call it—a plot plan?"

"Of course." Mrs. Thompson went to a cabinet, shuffled through her files and plucked out a sheet of paper. "We call this a lot card. This one is for the Gardner family mausoleum. It's a famous hillside tomb, right there on Auburn Lake. Isabella Stewart Gardner is buried there."

"Oh, right. I've seen them, rows of buildings set into the hill on both sides of the lake." Leonard looked at the plan, which showed only two rows of small rectangles inside a larger rectangle, and he thought at once, *reflective symmetry*. "Expensive properties, they must have been," he said, greatly daring.

"Oh, yes, I'm sure they were. Good Boston Brahmins, all along there. Coolidges, Cabots, Lodges, Higginsons, Kirklands. It's like another Beacon Street."

Leonard smiled. "They were just moving from the best address in Boston to the best in the cemetery." He asked his last nosy question. "Might I see the lot card for the Fell family plot?"

But Mrs. Thompson had come to the end of her permissiveness. "I'm sorry. You'll have to ask Eleanor Fell. No, that's wrong." She laughed, and they said it together, "Eleanor *Oliphant* Fell."

"May I have her phone number?"

Mrs. Thompson seemed to feel that as the representative of a prestigious institution serving the grieving survivors of the dead, she had already gone too far. "I suggest you try the telephone book," she said gently, and retreated to her desk.

30

THERE'S ANOTHER LETTER," MUTTERED LEONARD INTO his pocket phone. He was standing beneath the Egyptian gate, staring out at the traffic light on Mount Auburn Street. At once it turned green, and fifteen cars gathered speed and zoomed past him, heading east into Cambridge or west to Belmont and Watertown.

What did you say?" said Homer. "Speak up, Leonard."

"I said," croaked Leonard, "she's written him another

letter."

"Who do you mean, she? Oh, *she?* You mean it's another letter to Patrick?"

"Right. Wait a sec. I'll read it to you." Leonard fumbled in his pocket, unfolded the letter with difficulty and began to read it aloud.

A truck thundered by, racing to make the green light. A second truck, a third.

"Leonard, stop," roared Homer, "I can't hear a damn thing. Listen, we're coming. We'll be there in a jiffy." Leonard could hear him bellow something to Mary, and for a moment there was silence, and then Homer shouted into the phone again. "Sure, sure. Half an hour, Leonard. We'll be there in half an hour."

It would be their second visit to his attic apartment. The last time had been at night, and the grubbiness of various corners hadn't mattered. Now the afternoon sun was pouring in.

Leonard threw himself into the job of making his bed and washing a heap of dirty dishes. When he heard feet thumping up the stairs he snatched his pajamas from the back of a chair and stuffed them under a pillow. On his rush to the door he kicked a shoe out of the way and nearly fell over the brimming bucket. Shouting, "Just a minute," he hoisted the bucket into the sink, poured it out with a rush of dirty water and shoved it into a closet.

But Homer and Mary were charmed by his light-filled attic. "Wow," said Homer, admiring the display of prints tacked to the slanting ceiling. "It's like the Escher exhibition. Oh, say, I like this one, the dragon eating its own tail."

Mary went to the window and looked out. "Oh, Leonard, it's really nice here. Such a classy address. I wish we could find something like this."

Leonard was surprised. "You're moving to Cambridge?"

Mary glanced at Homer, who merely looked back at her gloomily. "It's the river bank, you see, Leonard," she said nervously, as if that summed the matter up.

"The river bank?"

Homer growled something indistinct, and Mary hastened to explain. "In the wintertime, you see, Leonard. I mean, that's the trouble. Listen, Leonard, there's this steep hill and it's really ghastly in January, so we really have to move, no question about it." Slapping her hands briskly, she turned to the window. "But we'll never find anything as nice as this."

"I was lucky," said Leonard gravely. He picked up the letter he had found at Patrick's grave. "Would you like to see—?"

But Mary was lost in contemplation of the rooftops and chimneys and back gardens and outbuildings and garages of the neighboring houses on Sibley Road. "You know, Leonard, it's hard to put into words, but there's something unique about these old Cambridge houses. What is it exactly, Homer? We've talked about it before."

Homer cheered up at once. "Everything dark brown, the Colosseum in faded sepia, the ruins of Pompeii."

"The complete works of Sir Walter Scott."

"Marble busts, Dante and Shakespeare."

"Hatracks and umbrella stands. Cuckoo clocks."

"Invalid aunts in darkened bedrooms."

Astonished, Leonard made a shy objection. "Well, sure, that's perfect for Mrs. Winthrop's house downstairs, but I don't know about the others—down the street, I mean."

"Oh, well, of course." Mary laughed and turned away

100

from the window. "They're not dark brown any more, of course they're not. They're apricot, I'll bet, with giant paintings on the wall, you know the kind, all red with one yellow stripe."

"But the ghostly presences," insisted Homer, "they're still there, I'll bet, all over the place. Old ectoplasmic professors seeping through the wallpaper. It's a known scientific fact that you can't get rid of ectoplasmic professors behind the wallpaper. They stay right there and peek out from time to time."

Leonard waved his letter feebly, but Homer was in full flight. "Or maybe it's the lay of the land around here. Think of it, all those nineteenth-century people had to climb the same steep hill, gasping for breath, and probably those old gasps are still here, circulating up and down and around and around, and of course the birds are just the same and the sun sets in exactly the same direction."

"Not exactly," murmured Leonard, "because of the precession of the equinoxes."

"What?" said Homer. "Oh, that." He shuddered, and sank into a chair. "Actually, the truth is, I've had my fill of ghostly presences. I mean, like all those phantoms floating around over Mount Auburn Cemetery. Enough's enough."

Leonard too was afflicted with ghosts. He looked down at his feet, shifted the toes of his shoes to line them up with the edge of a floorboard, and said nothing.

31

AT LAST MARY AND HOMER STOPPED TRYING TO
define the character of Leonard's neighborhood. They
sat down and looked at the new message from the dead
baby's lunatic mother.

"She's talking about some kind of spiritualist,"
guessed Mary, "this Madame Ronda."

Homer shook his head. "What a fruitcake."

"And there's something else." Leonard picked up a
folder and emptied its contents on his desk. A shower of
scraps fell out. "Snapshots, cut to pieces. They were on
the floor in Frieda's apartment. Look." He began putting
them together like a puzzle.

Homer and Mary watched as the puzzle turned into
people. Four people. There was a gaunt woman with
grey hair, a grinning child with yellow pigtails, a good-
looking woman with her blond hair swept stylishly
back, and a grave young woman with yellow hair cut
unstylishly short.

Leonard tapped the face of the young woman and
said, "Frieda."

Mary leaned over the pictures and said, "Oh, Homer,
look. I recognize this other one, the glamorous one. It's
Edward's niece. I told you, Homer, remember? We
think she killed her uncle by shoving his wheelchair
down the stairs. I mean the head nurse and I, that's what
we think. We saw it happen. And afterwards you and I
decided she must have been the babysitter."

"Edward's niece?" Leonard was confused. "You
mean Edward Fell? But I saw his grave just now. He's

just been buried next to Patrick."

"Well, of course, that figures," said Homer. "Edward Fell was Patrick's father."

Leonard's head was reeling. He gaped at Mary. "You mean you saw his death?"

Mary explained about the nursing home. "I visit a friend there. One of the other people was a senile old man in a wheelchair. I saw him there several times, Edward Fell."

Leonard was bewildered. "A senile old man was the baby's father?"

"Senile and old now," said Homer kindly, as if explaining to a child, "but not twelve years ago. And anyway, you're always hearing about hundred-year-old geezers dandling babies on their knees."

"And I also saw his niece," said Mary, pointing to the puzzle pieces. "There she is in person. And I could swear she was responsible for his death."

Leonard gazed at the disconnected fragments. "You mean," he said slowly, "she's Edward's niece, so in other words she's Patrick's cousin, so you think she was once the babysitter? But that means"—he pointed at the little girl—"could this be the same woman as a child? At the time of the accident that killed her cousin? The young babysitter herself?"

Homer stared at the puzzle pieces. "Then maybe this older woman was Patrick's mother, Edward's wife. But doesn't she look too old to have a child?"

"Not these days," said Mary. "What is she here? Forty-five? Fifty? It's not impossible."

"If those two go together," murmured Leonard, "then Frieda and the grown-up babysitter go together." He pushed the pieces around with his finger. "There are really only two pictures. They must have been taken years apart, but they're both in the same place. They're all standing in front of the same door."

Homer stared. "So which one goes with which?"

They shuffled them back and forth, making different combinations. "Mathematically," said Leonard, "there are four possible pairs."

"Right," said Homer. "One would be the little girl and the older woman, who is probably Edward's wife, the mother of Patrick."

"Or," said Leonard, "you could put together the older woman and Frieda."

"What about Edward's glamorpuss niece and the child?" said Mary.

"Which leaves Frieda and Glamorpuss," said Homer, "as possibility number four." He looked up at Mary. "The niece in the nursing home, did you get her name?"

"Oh, God," said Mary, "let me think. I asked Dorothy, the head nurse. I know she's a Fell, all right, but what was the rest? Oh, I remember, she's Eleanor Fell. With a couple of initials in the middle. Eleanor Something Something Fell."

"Oliphant," whispered Leonard. "Eleanor Oliphant Fell."

"Oh, Leonard," said Mary, "how do you know that?"

"Because she arranged for Edward's burial. Mrs. Thompson told me. You remember, Homer, Mrs. Thompson at the cemetery."

"Mrs. Thompson told you that? She told you the niece's middle name?"

"Yes, it's Oliphant. She said this Eleanor Fell is really proud of being an Oliphant. She's into the genealogy of her distinguished ancestors."

"Yes," said Mary, "I think one of her middle initials was an O. What was the other one?" She shook her head. "I can't remember." She brightened. "But Oliphant must be Patrick's middle name too. Remember? He was listed in the death records as Patrick O. Fell? So he must have been Patrick Oliphant Fell."

"Mmmm," said Homer, bending over the snipped pieces again, trying to nudge them sideways. "Have you tried this, Leonard? Maybe the edges will tell us how the scraps go together. I mean, sure, it's the same door, twelve years or so apart, but we ought to be able to see which goes with which."

But too much was missing. They couldn't match one side with another.

"Question," said Mary. "Why didn't Edward's wife ever come to visit her husband? She writes those letters, so we know she's still alive, but she never came to the nursing home. Edward's niece came to see him, but not his wife."

"Also," said Homer, "who took the pictures? And whose door is it? Maybe it's somebody else's door, like maybe it belongs to some other person, like a relative." He looked at Leonard, frowning. "And why did Frieda cut up the pictures and throw them away?"

Leonard shrugged his shoulders and shook his head.

Giving up simultaneously, they all sat down. "Okay then," said Mary, sinking into the sagging cushion of her chair, "what should we be doing? I mean from now on?"

"Well," said Homer, "I suppose the ultimate objective is not to pursue the niece for killing her uncle, but to find Leonard's girlfriend, right?"

"She's not my girlfriend," whispered Leonard, staring at his knees, which were crossed the wrong way. He crossed them the other way, but they still didn't feel right, and he put both feet on the floor.

"Well, whatever," said Homer heartlessly. "There she is, standing beside the aunt or the mother or somebody, so what relation does she have with any of them?"

"The phone book." Mary seized the arms of her chair and struggled to stand up. "Eleanor Oliphant Fell, the niece, she knows everything. We'll call her up."

"Sorry," said Leonard dryly, "I just tried that. I called Cambridge information, and they found an E. Fell, but the number's unlisted."

With a mighty effort Mary hurled herself out of her chair. "Well, there's still the mother. At least we can find Patrick's mother, because she keeps leaving those crazy letters at her little boy's grave. If we can only catch her there, we can find out who's who and what's what. And I'll bet she could tell us where to find Frieda." Mary looked keenly at Homer. "We've got to take turns in Mount Auburn, waiting for her to show up."

"Take turns?" Homer looked at her, aghast. He had suffered through long vigils before.

"At the cemetery. We've got to wait around there, hoping she'll come along."

"Oh, God," said Homer.

Leonard accompanied them downstairs and said goodbye. Then, thinking hard, he climbed slowly back up to his attic apartment, which was streaked with late afternoon sunshine, lighting up the puzzle pieces on his desk. A single ray shone like a spotlight on one of the Escher prints tacked to the slanting ceiling, the woodcut called *Other World*. It was a famous print incorporating three perspectives at once. Which world was which? Which way was up? It was a typical Escher puzzle.

Sitting down to his own puzzle, he huddled over the

106

scraps again, trying them in different combinations. This one with that one, that one with this one, which way was right?

In the car on the way home as they waited for the light to change at Aberdeen Street, Homer glanced at Mary and said, "Tell me, does he seem all right to you?"

"Who, Leonard? Well, no, he doesn't." Mary watched as a couple of young mothers pushed strollers across the intersection, heading for the pleasant paths and byways of the cemetery. "At least he's not the person we met that day in the crystal collection. He seems shrunken somehow. And his hair looks funny. And it's odd the way he keeps sitting with his legs crossed one way, and then he tries them the other way, as though he couldn't get comfortable. Maybe he's in pain. Maybe something's physically the matter."

As it happened, Leonard's sister had wondered the same thing when she dropped in on Leonard that morning. Hannah lived in Somerville and envied her brother his lucky attic on Sibley Road.

Afterward she called her mother in Cohasset. "He's so remote," said Hannah. "It's like he's living in a world of his own."

"He's always lived in a world of his own," said her mother. "What's wrong with that?"

"No, mother, it's worse than that."

"What do you mean worse?"

Hannah couldn't explain, but she could see it clearly. Something really weird was happening to her brother.

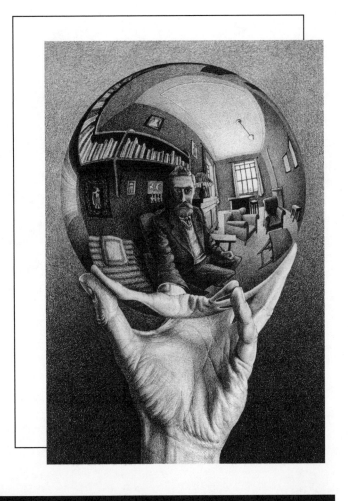

Hand with Reflecting Sphere

While drawing I sometimes feel as if I were a spiritualist medium...

M.C. Escher

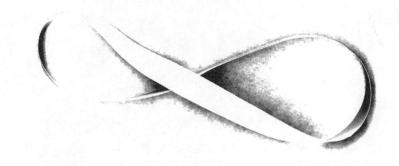

32

THE SIGN SAID—

GROTTO OF SAGITTARIUS
DONNA CARMELA, CLAIRVOYANT
PALM AND CRYSTAL READINGS

To the client the so-called grotto looked just right, not like the last place, which had been all wrong.

The room was dark and candlelit. Sparkling suns and moons hung from the ceiling, moving slightly in the warm air above the candles. A cloth woven with mystic patterns covered the table. In the center lay a crystal ball, sparkling with reflections of the candle flames. It was large and magisterial.

The client sat down and said at once, "I have two requests."

The woman across the table was robed in black. Her grey hair hung in strings, her eyes were smudged with mascara, her fingers glittered with rings.

The dark eyes flashed, examining the client. In a moment Donna Carmela said softly, "Name them."

Eagerly the client said, "Can you reach the souls of the departed?"

Again the eyes roved over the client's face. "Sometimes." Then Donna Carmela held up one hand and murmured, "Your other request?"

"I want to find someone."

The blackened eyelids closed, then opened. "The second shall come first. Describe the person."

"A young woman."

"Her appearance?"

"Homely, thin. Short dirty-blond hair, brown eyes, olive complexion. She's run away."

"She was in your care?"

"Well, no, not exactly." The client leaned forward and whispered, "She has a secret. A dark secret, known only to me. Once she—"

The ringed hand rose again. The smudged eyes closed. "Stop, I do not need to know. Let us look."

The client gasped. The crystal ball was beginning to glow, to rise from the table. The light within it grew brighter and brighter, and there was music, dim and shimmering, violins pizzicato.

"You are fortunate," whispered Madame Carmela, "to consult the crystal during the time of full moon. Last night I recharged it in the moonlight."

One by one the candles went out. Spirals of smoke rose upward and there was a smell of extinguished wax. Madame Carmela passed one hand over the ball, then the other. "I am magnetizing the crystal. Creating a link."

"A link?"

"Close your eyes. When you open them again, you will see clouds in the crystal, then flecks of gold."

The client closed her eyes, then opened them and stared at the glowing ball.

Madame Carmela was a fraud, but she was not a fool. Wryly she told herself that if anything were to appear in the center of her crystal ball it would be an image of her fierce and self-centered client. She was one of those people around whom the whole world turned.

But the client herself was satisfied. This was more like it. It was exactly what she had been looking for.

33

HOMER WAS SICK AND TIRED OF IT. THERE WAS
nothing of any consequence about the whole damned
thing. It was just a teensy piece of insanity on the part of
this otherwise intelligent young man. Leonard
Sheldrake had met this female person for only a fraction
of a second, so to speak. Why was he still so obsessed?

And now Homer's demanding wife expected him to
act like an idiot and spend the afternoon monitoring the
baby's grave.

"I haven't got time," he protested loudly. "I've got to
bone up on my old lecture notes because I've forgotten
all I ever knew about the European origins of New
England transcendentalism." He pointed an accusing
finger at Mary. "Okay, woman, tell me where in hell it
came from."

"Don't call me woman," said Mary. "And anyway—"

"You mean I can't call you either a female or a
woman? What are you, some kind of female
impersonator? Listen, my dear, I happen to have
personal private knowledge that you are a member of
the gentler sex. Although, I must say, gentle is hardly
the right word in your case."

Mary burst out laughing. "Oh, Homer, darling, it's
such a lovely day. You can bring a book along, study up
on the European origins of transcendentalism. We've
got Immanuel Kant around here somewhere. And, hey,
you could take the folding stool. Remember the folding
stool I bought in Venice?"

"The folding stool? Christ almighty." Homer glared
at his wife. "Why don't you go? Sit on the damned thing

113

yourself?"

"Oh, I'm sorry, dear, but it's Wednesday. I've got three seminars this afternoon, one right after the other. Whereas you, Homer, have the afternoon off."

❋

The folding stool was too close to the ground. When Homer lowered himself on it with gingerly care, the crisscrossed wooden legs burst at once and dumped him on the grass.

Laboriously he got to his feet and looked around for something to lean on, here on the low hill that overlooked baby Patrick's grave, thinking sourly that the only really interesting question in this cemetery was whether or not a telephone had been buried with Mary Baker Eddy. If so, did it ever ring? Was Elvis on the line?

An imposing monument to one Zachariah Winthrop was big enough to lean against, but its granite base was surrounded by begonias, leaving no room to sit down.

The chubby urn devoted to the Greenleaf family was adorned with a pious verse, *I heard a voice from heaven,* but it looked knobby and uncomfortable.

A tall pillar was promising. Homer sat down and tried to settle his bulk against the base of a monument dedicated to the memory of—

PHILIP MARETT
DIED MARCH 22, 1869, AGED 76
Founder of the New Haven Public Library

The man had obviously been a benefactor to the human race, but as a comfy sofa he was no good at all.

Homer struggled to his feet again and looked for a soft-looking place on the lawn. He found a grassy spot, sat down, unhitched his backpack and took out his old lecture notes on the European origins of New England transcendentalism.

The origins included a poem by Wordsworth. Homer remembered that part of the lecture with pleasure because of the passage about the sense sublime—

> —*a sense sublime*
> *Of something far more deeply interfused,*
> *Whose dwelling is the light of setting suns—*

Yes, yes, of course. But the rest was more difficult, philosophical treatises by Immanuel Kant, selections from the notebooks of Samuel Taylor Coleridge.

Homer bowed his head and dug into it. The breeze ruffled his hair, the sun dropped flickering images on the white paper. Someone coughed.

Homer looked up. Was it Patrick's mother? No, the little glen below his high perch was empty. He looked around, saw no one, and went back to his notes.

There was another cough.

Homer thought about it. Could he identify what language the invisible person was coughing in? No, of course not. Coughing was part of a universal language that included—Homer smiled and made a list in his head—

chuckling
laughing
giggling
tittering
sniffling
sobbing

weeping
moaning
screaming
howling
roaring—

He heard a sneeze, and added it to the list—

sneezing
hissing
growling
sputtering
snoring
snorting
belching
gasping
hiccupping

They were all animal noises like barking and purring, the same in every tongue. Homer preened himself on this new discovery. He might write a paper on *The Esperanto of Nonverbal Speech,* and deliver it to the American Philological Society.

"Excuse me."

Homer looked around in surprise. This time the language was English.

An old woman was looking at him. Her eyes were wide, her smile was sweet. A folded newspaper was tucked under her arm.

Homer rose to his feet, the perfect gentleman, bowed slightly and said, "Good afternoon, Ma'am."

Mrs. Winthrop put out one hand in kindly sympathy and touched his sleeve. "Have you lost someone dear to you? Has a loved one crossed the bridge to the other side?"

"Crossed the bridge?" Homer was confused for a moment, but then he hastened to explain himself. "No, no, I was just—I mean it's so peaceful here. I was reading."

"You've chosen such a lovely neighborhood," said Mrs. Winthrop. "There are so many truly interesting men and women here on Willow Avenue. It makes a loop, you see." She drew a circle in the air. "It goes around and around."

She took his arm and drew him along, introducing him to the local residents one by one, beginning with her own eminent husband, Zachariah, then going on to the Lowells and the Norcrosses and James Bryant Conant, a president of Harvard.

Homer was stunned by a tall triangular monument. "Who's this?"

"Oh, the Mountforts," gushed Mrs. Winthrop. "I think of them as triangles, with funny little arms and legs." She giggled, and Homer was charmed. Then Mrs. Winthrop pointed vaguely to the east. "And Mrs. Gardner is just down there."

"Mrs. Gardner? You mean Isabella Stewart Gardner?"

"My mother was invited to one of her garden parties," said Mrs. Winthrop proudly. "There were Japanese lanterns and tiny triangular sandwiches. Oh!"—she made a joke—"the Mountforts should have been there!"

Homer laughed and took her hand. The old lady was a dear. "Thank you, Mrs. Winthrop." She was fluttering away, and he called after her, "I hope we meet again."

But the afternoon had been a failure. The baby's mother had not put in an appearance and the importance of Immanuel Kant to the flowering of New England transcendentalism was still a mystery.

117

34

FRIEDA'S NEW APARTMENT WAS EVEN GRUBBIER THAN the old one, but she got to work at once with a paintbrush. Before long the smeared walls of the room looking out on the impacted intersection of Inman Square were bright and white, and she was beginning to work on the kitchen.

As a furnished apartment it was no worse than her old place on lower Sibley Road. Frieda made it her own by tacking up a poster of her favorite Escher print, part of the long woodcut called *Metamorphosis*. The poster showed the end of the woodcut, the part in which a chessboard turns into a city. The clever transition, the delightful metamorphosis, was the little bridge that reached across the water to the city from a tower that was also a rook on the chessboard.

Frieda's new apartment was her rook, her tower, her stronghold of anonymity. Her absentminded landlord had not questioned his tenant's new name, Frances Pole, and neither had the telephone company. Perhaps some day she would leave the tower and cross the bridge and reach the beautiful city, but not yet.

Inman Square was far from beautiful, but Frieda found a job around the corner as a file clerk for a wholesale distributor of manila envelopes. Her co-workers were neither highly educated nor artistically skillful, but they had the same range of human strengths and frailties as the friends of her former life, and some were wiser and funnier than the people she had known before.

So it was all right. If only she could stay here quietly.

If only the old witch would leave her alone.

Frieda had written no more letters to the Impossible Post Office. When her first actual letter had remained unanswered—the genuine friendly letter that she had sent through the United States Postal Service to a real person with a real address—she had felt silly and ashamed.

So these days, if she ever thought about someone named Leonard, a short grey man in a checkered scarf, she shoved the thought aside. Of course it is hard not to think about something. Frieda devoted a good deal of time to the practice of not thinking.

Today she was ready to tackle the kitchen ceiling. Frieda spread old newspapers on the floor and knelt to stir her can of paint. Only then did she see the name staring up at her from a page of death notices—

EDWARD FELL, 68

At once she was struck with painful memories. *Edward Fell!* How kind he had always been to her, what a bulwark and defender! But gradually the bulwark had vanished as his growing confusion became more desperate and his wife gained a freer hand.

Poor Edward! He had really died years ago. Perhaps his actual death could be called a blessing.

35

HOMER WAS DOUBTFUL. "SPIRITUALISTS WITH CRYSTAL balls? There can't be people like that any more."

"Oh, yes, there are," said Mary. "They're all over the place. I'll bet we can find Madame Ronda."

And they did. In the yellow pages the heading for spiritualists was between spiral staircases and sponges.

To Homer's surprise there were many listings. One was exactly what they were looking for.

> Aquarian Truth Center of Light
> Astral Images
> Chloe's Labyrinth
> Goddessworks
> Grotto of Sagittarius
> Madame Ronda
>   SEE OUR DISPLAY AD THIS PAGE
> Sun, Moon and Stars
> Zodiac Power

The display ad for Madame Ronda was a staring eye looking out from the palm of an open hand with the words—

PSYCHIC READINGS
BY MME RONDA

•

PALMISTRY
TAROT CARDS

•

Walk-ins Welcome
1039 Norfolk St., Central Sq. Camb.

"It's up to you, dear," said Homer. "It's your kind of thing."

Mary was incensed. "What do you mean, my kind of thing?"

"Oh, you know," said Homer uncomfortably. "Witches, they're female, and so are gypsy fortune-

120

tellers. Female irrationality and hysteria, right up your alley." Mary's mouth fell open, and Homer finished lamely, "Joke, that's a joke."

"Well, all right," said Mary, giving in. "I guess I'm curious anyway." She poked him in the chest. "But listen, Homer, if we're going to put the house on the market, why don't you work on the cellar while I'm gone? We've got to get rid of all that old stuff down there, although I don't know what on earth you can possibly do with it, now that the old dump is gone."

"The dear old dump," said Homer dreamily. "All those bashed-in refrigerators and mountains of plastic bags. Ah, the dear dead days of the past."

Central Square was Cambridge in transition. Mary Kelly was aware that Emily Dickinson had once lived in exile only a few blocks away, suffering from eye trouble and homesickness in a darkened room.

But nothing of an Emily Dickinson aesthetic pervaded this part of Massachusetts Avenue. Only a mile from Harvard Square, it might have been in Moscow.

For Homer and Mary Kelly the other choked intersection was home ground, the knotted angle where the brick walls of Harvard University crowded up against the curve of Massachusetts Avenue. Harvard Square was crisscrossed by Ph.D. candidates and professors, students and street people, kids on scooters and skates, burly teenagers from the public high school on the other side of Harvard Yard, pavement musicians with open guitar cases, hawkers of the homeless newspaper *Spare Change,* noisy Peruvian bands, booksellers and bookbuyers, shoppers at the Gap, restaurants dishing up arugula and fennel, and five hundred miscellaneous poets.

In Central Square the throngs on the sidewalk were scruffier and more mixed in race and country of origin. In the old days of rent control, new immigrants had once been thick on the streets, but now the high cost of living had forced many of the city's poor to move elsewhere. Here and there a few buildings had been taken over by nonprofit developers, but only for the benefit of a few hundred elderly people.

The subway stop was twenty feet below the intersection of Massachusetts Avenue with Western Avenue, River and Magazine Streets. Mary climbed the dark stairs into air and sky. Around her there were milling crowds of pedestrians. Some gazed at the tormented traffic lights, some crossed daringly from corner to corner, dodging the trucks and delivery vans and cars turning in four or five different directions. A block away from the intersection rose the tower of City Hall, high above Massachusetts Avenue. Southward on River Street the steeple of an enormous church was a relic from a different age.

Where was Madame Ronda? As Mary looked at her map, a big man in a knitted cap said boldly, "Hey, ma'am, you got a dollar?"

In a fraction of a second Mary's lifetime accumulation of social history and ethical principle funneled down into a decision to grope in her pocketbook and extract a bill. The man took it without a word and shambled away.

Leonard Sheldrake had explained it on the phone, the layout of Central Square. "It's really four different towns—Area Four, Cambridgeport, Riverside and Mid-Cambridge. Area Four used to be the grungiest, but now it's being gentrified along with the rest. And M.I.T. has a few big projects in Area Four. They play the City Council like a violin."

Mary started walking in the direction of Norfolk Street, glancing at the shopfronts—*Tax Man, Burger King, Goodwill, Center for Marxist Education, Cambridge Business Center, the Salvation Army.* Along Mass Av the city planners had been at work. There were trees encircled with wrought-iron fences, there were benches under the trees. Norfolk Street was more neglected. Much of the upgrading here had been do-it-yourself. Salesmen for vinyl siding had been busy too. They had scampered up and down from block to block, covering rotting wooden clapboards with phony siding and nailing up plastic shutters.

Mary found the emporium of Madame Ronda del Rondo across the street from the Faithful and True Witness Apostolic Church of Jesus Christ. It was flanked by Anita's Caribbean American Grocery (*Hablamos Espanol*) and the Haitian Express Bureau de Transfer.

The door opened on a stairway. Beside the stairs stood a large wooden hand like the one in the telephone book. On the five fingers were the words, HEALTH, MONEY, FRIENDS, RELATIONS, LOVE.

So far, so good. Mary walked bravely up the stairs, composing in her head a story about her interest in the other world. At the top she was surprised to find herself in a big airy room. A young man sat before a computer monitor, jouncing a whimpering baby in his lap.

"Oh, hi, there," he said. "You want to see my mother? Wait a sec." He stood up, holding the baby against his shoulder. At once a beautiful young woman appeared from nowhere with another baby in her arms.

"Lena's turn now," she said, and they traded armfuls.

123

"Twins?" said Mary, amused.

"Right," said the father. "This is Lena." He nodded at his wife, who was vanishing with the other baby. "That's Lola."

"Is your wife Madame Ronda?"

"No, no. Madame Ronda's my mother." He gestured at an open door. "She'll see you in there." He sat down at the computer again with Lena fast asleep on his lap, and grinned at Mary. "Now maybe I can get some work done."

"You're a computer—uh—programmer?"

"It's our website. I'm the one keeps it up."

"Oh, I see." Obediently Mary walked through the door and sat down in Madame Ronda's consulting chamber. To her surprise it looked more like a doctor's waiting room than a den of mystery. There were no heavy draperies. The room was bright with sunlight. There was no atmosphere of the occult, no crystal ball.

When Madame Ronda sailed in, holding out her hand, Mary shook it and made a laughing confession. "It's not what I expected at all. I thought it would be all dark and mysterious."

Madame Ronda smiled and sat down comfortably in an upholstered chair. She was a large handsome woman. Mary noticed with relief that her beautiful dark eyes did not widen and stare and cast a mesmerizing spell.

"How can I help you?" asked Madame Ronda kindly.

Mary told the truth. "I want to ask about—um—a client of yours. She—"

"I'm sorry," said Madame Ronda, interrupting at once and shaking her head. "I cannot discuss private conversations. They are confidential."

"Oh, I see." Mary thought a moment, and tried another tack. "Suppose someone came to you wanting

124

to communicate with a relative who had passed away. Would you be able to help? What would you do?"

"I would tell the bereaved person that the spirit of the departed is now at rest. I would try to help the seeker find peace of mind."

"That's all? You wouldn't go into a trance and summon the voice of the deceased?"

"No, nothing like that. My aim would be to help the grieving relative adjust to life in the real world. I might urge her to find other interests."

Mary was stunned. She caught at a word. "Her? You mean a woman? Are you thinking of a particular woman?"

"No, no. It's just that most of my clients are women."

There was another pause. It was not embarrassing. Madame Ronda sat quietly, faintly smiling.

Mary abandoned her attempt to probe the strange secret life of the mother of Patrick Fell, and asked a more general question. "You're a gypsy, Madame Ronda? Are most psychics gypsies? Tell me, are gypsies professing Christians?"

In answer Madame Ronda leaned forward and told a story. "The Bible says that five nails were driven into the body of Christ. Gypsies say that a sixth was meant for his heart, but we stole it."

"You stole it? You mean gypsies stole the sixth nail?" Mary laughed with delight.

Madame Ronda laughed too. "We are Catholics. My family belongs to the parish of The Blessed Sacrament on Pearl Street."

After this respite from hard questions, Mary thought of another. "Suppose I came to you with a desire to communicate with—say, a dead child. And then I was disappointed when you told me that you wouldn't try to invoke his spirit in the other world. Suppose I didn't want to give up. Maybe I'd want to try someone else, you know, get a second opinion. Would it be possible to find more traditional psychics? You know, the stereotype, with crystal balls and so on?"

"Oh, yes, I suppose it would be possible."

"But where? How?"

Madame Ronda opened her mouth to reply, but there was a noisy interruption. Her daughter-in-law hurried in, her face wet with tears. She was carrying one of the twins. It was bawling lustily.

Madame Ronda held out her arms and enfolded the baby and cuddled it and made soft cooing noises. At once the baby—was it Lena or Lola?—stopped crying and gazed adoringly at its grandmother.

"Oh, thank you, thank you," sobbed the daughter-in-law. "Honestly, I've really had it. If it isn't one, it's the other."

"There, there, dear. Lie down and rest. Lola and I will be fine."

Mary stood up. "Can you tell me where else someone might go, if they wanted a different sort of help?"

There was a cry from the other room. Baby Lena, too, was getting up a head of steam. Madame Ronda rose majestically with Lola in her arms, and Mary followed her out of the consulting room. She watched as the grandmother swept up the other baby from the embrace of its exasperated father. Holding the two babies in her arms like a goddess of fertility, she looked at Mary and said, "What did you say, dear?"

"Nothing," said Mary. "Thank you so much. Those babies are really cute."

"Madame Ronda, I really liked her."

126

Homer was flabbergasted. "You *liked* her?"

"Oh, yes, she was just great. I wanted to tell her all my troubles."

"Troubles?" Homer was wounded to the quick. "What troubles?"

"Oh, you know, Homer. It's just a figure of speech. But really, she wasn't what I expected at all. I wanted to sit on her lap and suck my thumb."

36

HOMER AND MARY KELLY AND LEONARD SHELDRAKE— all three were employed by the university that bulged eastward from Harvard Square, the institution Homer called *that vast educational slaughterhouse,* in the words of H. L. Mencken.

To their joint relief, the spring term was over. Leonard's freedom would last the longest, an entire sabbatical year. Nevertheless he was dangerously available to his department chairwoman. Joanna knew his e-mail address as well as the number of his unlisted phone.

She was in raptures, she said, over his computer program for beginning students. She adored the way his rhombohedrons and scalenohedrons turned slowly on the screen; she was delighted with his demonstration of left-handed and right-handed trigonal trapezohedrons; she was enchanted by his display of the fantastic intergrowth of the twinned cubes of fluorite. "Oh, Leonard, it's just like holding a tourmaline from Namibia in your hand, or an alexandrite from the Ural Mountains. I can almost explore the facets with my fingers. It's so wonderful, the way they blink and flash in the light."

But this triumph wasn't enough. "Leonard, you've got to do crystal systems right away. Please, Leonard! We'd all be so grateful."

For Homer and Mary, too, the end of the semester did not mean the end of drudgery. Mary had to write a speech for a summer conference. Homer was working on a book with a thousand footnotes. Therefore Leonard's anxiety about the disappearance of the young woman called Frieda would have to wait, along with questions about her mysterious connection with a long-dead child and the possible murder of an old man in a nursing home by his niece and the puzzling absence of the baby's mother, a madwoman who was trying to communicate with the dead.

Of course it was different for Leonard. No matter how busy he was, he could always find time to visit the art gallery on Huron Avenue, hoping to find Frieda there.

By necessity he was now a regular client of the elegant grocery store next door, buying his meager supplies at whatever cost—two fifty for a head of Boston lettuce, four dollars for a dozen treasures laid by happy chickens roaming free, pausing now and then to lay an egg.

So it was an expensive exercise, visiting the gallery nearly every day.

"Well, here you are again," marveled the gallery owner, as Leonard walked in for the umpteenth time. "But excuse me, perhaps I'm mistaking you for someone else. You've been here before?"

"Of course I have."

The gallery owner was embarrassed. "Oh, well, of

course. Anyway, take a good look because it's the last day. Are you interested in Budgie at all?"

"Budgie?"

"Oh, you must know Budgie's work. Trash cans, towers of trash cans. He piles them up so they sort of sway." The gallery owner's hands tipped left and right. "It's amazing. I mean they teeter as if they're going to fall on you. I don't know how he does it. It's truly remarkable. We're installing his stuff tomorrow."

"Well, I guess not," said Leonard. Turning away, he signed the guestbook, because it was an excuse to look back over the pages, hoping to find Frieda's name.

As always it was missing, but for some reason—perhaps the fact that it was the last day of the exhibition—he remembered something he had forgotten. On the opening day, when he had asked about a woman in a green coat, the gallery owner had said, "You mean two women in green coats?"

Two women! Who was the other?

That night Leonard dreamed that two Friedas in green coats were climbing out of their magic mirrors and changing places.

"Wait," he whispered, but they paid no attention. Both were striding away, growing smaller and smaller, disappearing at last in twin cavities of darkness.

His whisper woke him up, and he lay flat on his back staring at the rectangle of light on the ceiling, tossed up by a street lamp down there on Sibley Road.

There were two labyrinths, not just one. Who in the hell was the other Frieda?

37

BUSY OR NOT, MARY TRIED AGAIN TO FIND PATRICK'S mother by consulting the list of psychics in the yellow pages.

From the list that looked so strangely out of place on the same page as speech pathologists, speedometers, and sporting goods, she picked a name at random, *Madame Chloe.* And on the day after she finished the script for her *hugely important* keynote address, Mary celebrated by taking the T to Downtown Crossing to look for Madame Chloe.

Fortunately the address in the phone book was real. Beside the street number, an arrow pointed downward to a door below the level of the sidewalk. On the arrow were the words CHLOE'S LABARINTH.

At the bottom of the stairs a second sign was tacked to the door. It was another gallant try at a possible spelling—

CHLOE'S LABERYNTH

Mary knocked.

Nothing happened. She was about to give up when there was a scuffling on the other side of the door and it opened to reveal Madame Chloe in person, a teenager with a snub nose, a tiny mouth and large frightened eyes. She was struggling to knot a kerchief around her hair.

A cornered rabbit, thought Mary. "Are you open today?" she said politely.

"Well, I guess so," said Madame Chloe doubtfully. She backed away to let her client come in, then furtively snatched a shawl from the back of a chair and draped it over her T-shirt, which was emblazoned with the name of a rock band—

The Soft White Underbelly

Mary had encountered the Underbelly before. Smiling, she sat down on the rickety chair Madame Chloe jerked out for her. As a psychic studio the place looked reasonable enough. It sported a generic crystal ball on the table, and there were bits of astrological paraphernalia dangling from the pipes. Where was the labyrinth?

Mary waited for its proprietor to sit down on the other side of the table, but Madame Chloe remained standing. Mary looked up at her and asked her question without ceremony. "Tell me, Madame Chloe, can you communicate with the other side? With people who have passed on?"

Madame Chloe's kerchief was sliding off her hair. She grabbed it with both hands and rammed it down over her forehead. There was another pause. At last she said, "Mostly people just walk the labyrinth."

"Oh." Mary tried again. "The truth is, I'm looking for someone. Can you tell me whether or not a bereaved mother has consulted you recently, hoping to get in touch with her deceased baby boy?"

The rabbit bit her tiny lip and hitched up her shawl.

"It would be a kindness," said Mary, "if you could tell me. You see, I'm trying to find her because she's mentally ill."

But Madame Chloe had only one thought in her head. She made vague paddling motions with her hands and said, "My labyrinth. Most people—"

"Oh, all right." Mary stood up. "Where is it?"

At once Madame Chloe brightened. "You have to pay first," she said. "Five dollars."

Mary's serious attempt to find Patrick's mother had become a fascinated inspection of a strange cranny at the remote edge of the rational world. Reaching into her bag, she counted out five one-dollar bills.

"It's in here," said Madame Chloe. She swept aside a hanging bedspread and pulled the string of a bulb, dimly illuminating one corner of a cavernous cellar.

"I'm sorry," said Mary. "I don't see it."

"Look down."

The labyrinth was a nine-by-twelve rug. Machine-made, guessed Mary, probably in Battle Creek, Michigan, right next to the cornflakes factory. It had a commonplace spiraling pattern of flowers.

"Well, thank you," said Mary. "I guess I won't walk it today."

The spell, if it could be called that, was broken. Abruptly Madame Chloe turned and tripped over her shawl.

"I've had it," said Mary crossly. "No more spiritualists. It wouldn't get us anywhere anyway."

"Well, okay," said Homer. "That's all right with me.

38

Beech Avenue, Mount Auburn Cemetery, 10 A.M.

PUSHING BILLY'S STROLLER SLOWLY UP THE HILL, THE young mother saw the woman in the green coat emerge from Daisy Path and walk toward her. The woman was youngish, not likely to stop and coo over the baby the way old ladies so often did.

But there was a look in her eye that Billy's mother recognized. The woman in the green coat was approaching quickly and staring at Billy with that familiar *oh-what-a-cute-baby* look.

"Oh, what a cute baby," she said, stopping in front of them, blocking the way. "How old is he?"

At first Billy's mother didn't mind. In fact she liked it when strangers were charmed by her beautiful boy. "Fourteen months."

The woman bent down, chuckling, and gave Billy's tummy a gentle poke. The baby gurgled. "Oh, you must be so proud of him. Such a chubby little darling. May I pick him up? I just want to feel his fat little cheek against mine."

"Hey, wait a minute."

210 Aberdeen Street, second floor apartment, 11 A.M.

"Before I knew what was happening, she had him unstrapped. It was unbelievable. She was clutching him and starting to walk away down the hill, jabbering about how adorable he was. Incredible! I ran after her and said, 'Excuse *me*,' and tried to take him back, but she hung on, and Billy started yelling, and then she let go so suddenly I almost dropped him. And you know what she said?"

"God, no, what?"

"She said, 'Oh, I just adore babies. You see, there was a tragedy. I lost my own little darling.' So I said, 'Well, I'm *sorry*. But you can't have mine.' "

"Well, good for you. My God, people like that should

133

be incarcerated. Listen, from now on, don't take him there any more."

"Of course I won't. And anyway, it's so easy to get lost. You feel as if you're going around and around and never getting anywhere. It's like you're stuck in one dimension with all those dead people. I mean, it's really weird."

39

THIS TIME IT WAS HOMER WHO FOUND A LETTER IN THE metal box in the bushes, because it was his own infuriating turn again. It should have been Mary's graveyard watch, but she had unfairly squirmed out of it by pleading an appointment with a Concord real estate person.

But the truth was that Homer had no wish to be present at the loss of their house in Arcadia. He was glad he had an excuse to be somewhere else. In fact he planned to conduct an experiment in the cemetery by lying flat on his back on the grass and counting all the leaves on a tree. He had figured out a clever way to do it.

But first he poked in the crazy mailbox behind baby Patrick's small headstone. To his surprise he found another letter. A very recent letter. Whereas the earlier ones had been wilted and a little damp, this one looked crisp and fresh. The envelope was dry, the inked words were clear and sharp, not blurred with moisture.

The damn woman must have been here only a little while ago. Had she been one of the people he had passed on Central Avenue and Beech? There had been brisk walkers, mothers pushing baby buggys, a feisty old woman in hiking boots and a couple of people with field glasses. Those guys with binoculars would be looking for mauve-breasted skeets and lesser flutterbills and a lot of other peculiar species winging up from the southern hemisphere. And there'd be plenty of them, because the poor birds must be so exhausted. They'd be twittering joyfully and coming down in flocks to rest in the trees in this arboreal paradise.

The letter was even nuttier than usual.

Darling Boy!

My new contact was so helpful! She pounced at once on the crime itself. And she told me how dreadfully uneasy you are, how anxious that justice should be done after so many years.

Oh Patrick! To think what was taken from me! After so many failures you were such a blessing, such a gift! The doctor said you were the cutest and smartest baby she had ever seen! Therefore I am more determined than ever. At my next appointment I'll ask the crucial question, WHERE IS SHE?

Your loving Mother

As he lay down on his back for the great experiment of counting all the leaves on the tree that spread its branches wide and high above his head, Homer wondered what Patrick's insane mother thought was happening to the letters they had removed from the box.

Well, no problem. Anybody crazy enough to write sepulchral letters to the dead would also be crazy enough to think they had actually been delivered. Some angel, probably, had stooped down from heaven to pick them up, tucking them into a diaphanous pocket.

Or maybe it was the local mailman. Homer had run across his monument up there on Pyrola Path—

BARNABAS BATES
1787–1854
Founder of Cheap Postage

Maybe Barnabas was the postal go-between with the other world.

Counting all the leaves on a tree was easy. Nothing to it. Homer began with the nearest twig, on which there were six leaves. Okay, how many twigs on this little branchlet? Call it eight, so that was forty-eight leaves, call it fifty. There were about ten branchlets on the larger secondary branch, so that was five hundred, and there were fifteen secondary branches on the bigger branch, so that was—um—seventy-five hundred leaves on the first big branch altogether. Now, how many big branches were there on the whole entire tree from top to bottom? Say, fifty?

Homer grinned, making his final calculation. It turned out, after only five minutes of calculated guesses, that this tree, spreading so enormously over his head, shading his face so kindly from the sun, was a burgeoning universe of three hundred and seventy-five thousand leaves, give or take a few thousand.

He smirked. Who else would think of such a charmingly clever way to count all the leaves on an entire tree? Homer promised himself that the very next time they went to the beach he'd count all the grains of sand.

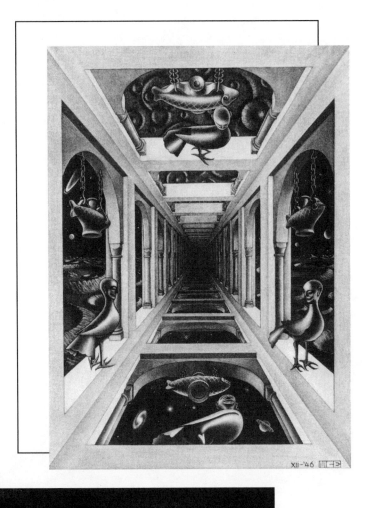

Other World

. . . suddenly to become aware. . . how mysterious
life is . . .
M.C.Escher

40

"COME TO OUR HOUSE THIS TIME," SAID MARY KELLY.

Well, okay," said Leonard. "Where is it?"

"It's a little tricky. You go out Route 2, but then you can't turn left on Fair Haven Road, so you have to go past it to the traffic light and reverse direction. And then— listen, Leonard—Fair Haven turns into a dirt road with a lot of forks. You have to take the right fork. I'll explain."

While Leonard listened he shifted the phone book in the telephone booth so that it made a perfect right angle with the edge of the shelf, and began lining up his coins in a row. "Two rights and a left," he mumbled, repeating Mary's directions and nudging a quarter with his thumb.

The appointment was for four-thirty, so he barely had time to race from the library at M. I. T. to the subway stop at Kendall Square and ride the T to Harvard, then take a cab to Sibley Road to pick up his car.

He hadn't counted on a moment of panic on the platform at Kendall Square. Staring like everybody else into the darkness of the tunnel, watching for the arrival of the train, Leonard was overcome by the sense that he had fallen into a frightening fantasy by M. C. Escher.

When the train appeared at last, humming pleasantly out of the darkness, its cheerful windows all alight, he boarded it thankfully.

"Oh, Leonard," said Mary, running down the porch steps, "I'm afraid our house is a mess. We're trying to clear out a lot of old stuff."

"It's Mary's fault," said Homer amiably, holding open the front door. "That woman never throws anything away."

Mary laughed. "Don't listen to him, Leonard. Come in and sit down." She put her foot on a cardboard box and shoved it across the room. Homer picked up another box and dumped it in the corner.

"You're really moving to Cambridge?" Leonard stared at the view out the window, where the great bend of the Sudbury River spread wide in a glittering lake. "What for? How can you leave all this behind?"

There was a short silence. Mary gave an embarrassed laugh. "The truth is, Homer doesn't want to move. It's my idea, I'm afraid."

"Oh, I see."

Homer grumbled something under his breath, and Leonard said doubtfully, "Well, I hope you find something. Cambridge real estate has gone through the roof."

"Tell me about it," said Homer gloomily.

They pulled their chairs close together and Homer read aloud the newest crazy letter from Patrick's mother.

They passed it from hand to hand.

"It reminds me of the film," said Mary. "The one of the baby's grave. There's the same sense of threat."

"This word 'justice,' " said Homer. "What does she mean, 'justice should be done'?"

"Vengeance," said Mary angrily. "She wants vengeance. That's what she means by justice."

"Vengeance," agreed Homer. "Vengeance on her niece, the babysitter."

Thinking of the woman she had seen in the nursing home, Mary and bitterly, "A lovely family, the whole clan. Especially the niece. First she killed the baby and then, years later, she killed her old Uncle Edward by pushing his wheelchair down a set of concrete stairs."

"Is there a pattern here?" said Homer. "We've got aunts, uncles, mothers, nieces, babysitters, babies, missing females and—"

"Homer!"

"Oh, sorry, not females."

Leonard gazed into his empty glass. "It's like the pattern of prime numbers. Aunts and uncles and so on. Elusive, like understanding the separations between primes. Just when you think there's a pattern, it surprises you."

"Sorry, Leonard," said Homer humbly. "I forget what they are, prime numbers."

Leonard took out a pencil, and soon they were bent over a scrap of paper on the coffee table. "You see, even the simplest sequences have deep and beautiful properties."

"Beautiful?" Homer stared at the scribbled numbers. "Well, okay, if you say so."

"Hey," said Mary, "What about the deep and beautiful properties of aunts and uncles?"

"That's right," said Homer, looking keenly at Leonard. "What's the pattern of the prime numbers in this case? I mean the prime suspects?"

"Two missing people," said Mary. "Frieda for one, and the crazy mother who writes the letters."

"And the niece," said Leonard. "Don't forget the niece." There were magazines heaped on the coffee table beside Leonard's glass, and he stacked them into a cube.

"You know," said Mary, taking the letter, "this part is really important—*After so many failures you were such a blessing.* I'll bet those failures were miscarriages." She looked up in triumph. "She had a long succession of

141

miscarriages, until at last this cutest of all babies was born." Shuddering, Mary looked back at the letter. "I wonder who this doctor was."

"What really seems sick to me," whispered Leonard, "is her belief that the baby himself is calling for vengeance."

"It's not just sick," said Homer, "it's scary."

"You know," said Leonard slowly, "there are specialists in difficult pregnancies. Maybe we could find the one who helped her."

"Brilliant," said Mary. She jumped up, leaped over a box of books, snatched up the Yellow Pages and plumped herself down beside Leonard on the sofa.

"Try physicians," he said softly.

She flipped the pages. "Here they are. Look, they're organized by specialty. What do we want, obstetrics?"

Leonard pointed to the heading, OBSTETRICS AND GYNECOLOGY.

"Good grief," said Mary, "what a lot of baby doctors."

"Well, the race gotta be reproduced," said Homer, getting up and reaching for the whiskey bottle. He held it over Leonard's glass. "A little more, Leonard? No? Mary? No? How about you, Homer? Well, yes, I don't mind if I do." He poured himself a refill, then craned his neck to stare at the densely printed pages of obstetricians. "You know what? I'll bet they don't have six pages of baby doctors in New Guinea."

"Oh, of course not," said Mary. "Those brave women in New Guinea go out to hoe the field in the morning, take a ten-minute break to deliver a baby, then go right back to work. What an inspiring example for the self-indulgent women of the Western world!"

41

IT WAS LEONARD WHO SUGGESTED TRYING THE subheading, *High Risk Pregnancies.*

The list of doctors was short. "This one sounds promising," said Mary, "Obstetrical Specialist Rosalind Rosebush at Emerson Hospital. Why don't I try her right now?"

Leonard coughed and stood up. "I'm sorry, but I've got to go."

Homer was disappointed. "We thought you were staying for supper."

"I'm insulted, Leonard," said Mary. "You've got something against my pasta?"

"No, no," mumbled Leonard, "it's just that—I'm sorry." On his way to the door he tripped over a box of Homer's big shoes. "Thank you again."

"Poor Leonard," said Homer, watching his car growl up the hill in low gear. "His wits are in good shape, but something else is astray. Do you think he's just a lovelorn fool, pining away for Frieda?"

"It's his hair," said Mary wisely. "That's what it is. He can't do anything with his hair."

As usual they had an argument about who was to take the time to visit Doctor Rosebush.

"Homer, why does it have to be me? Oh, I know." Mary turned sarcastic. "I suppose it's because I'm a female. Listen, Homer, you may remember that I've never actually had a baby myself, and therefore I know as little about the practice of obstetrics as any lordly male."

"But that sister of yours had such a teeming womb.

When I met you for the first time you were knee-deep in her offspring, and if I remember correctly, another member of the litter was on its way at the time. And aren't some of Gwen's daughters having babies themselves?"

"Yes, but that doesn't mean—" Mary stopped objecting, because of course it was true. Tenderly she remembered the long nights last fall when she had walked the floor with one of the babies.

"And Benny," cried Homer. "How can you forget Benny?"

Benny was the last of Gwen's children, a clever boy who had lived for half his young life with his Aunt Mary and Uncle Homer—a lovable but exhausting child.

"Well, okay then," said Mary, giving in. "I'll try this Rosebush woman, but she's probably not the right one."

As it turned out, Doctor Rosebush was indeed the right one. But when Mary walked into her office she gave the doctor a turn.

Well, of course, thought Doctor Rosebush, *the new techniques of fertility enhancement have been fairly successful with older women, so perhaps this will turn out to be an interesting case.* "Sit down, Ms."—she looked at her daybook—"Kelly. Am I right in assuming that your pregnancy is at risk?"

Mary laughed. "Oh, Doctor Rosebush, it isn't my pregnancy. I'm inquiring about someone else's."

"Someone else's? Your daughter's?"

"No, no." Mary leaned forward and explained. "I'm trying to find a woman who had a number of miscarriages some years ago, before finally giving birth to a healthy baby boy. Unfortunately the child was

144

killed in an accident later on. I wonder if she might have been a patient of yours?"

Doctor Rosebush looked at her soberly, then stood up and walked to the window, which looked out on a loading platform. "I'm sorry. I can't talk about private cases without the permission of the patient herself. It's not only unethical, it's illegal." She turned and looked gravely at the visitor. "What was her name?"

"We think it was Fell. But she may have used another name."

After another pause, Dr. Rosebush asked uneasily, "Is this a police matter?"

"Well, sort of. Not exactly." Mary had often wished that she had a little of her husband's shameless audacity. For years Homer had been flashing an antique identification card, left over from the days when he had been a lieutenant detective in the office of the district attorney of Middlesex County. Recently Homer had enclosed the dogeared card in plastic, so that it looked as good as new. At moments of crisis he was apt to whisk it out of his pocket, flourish it for a second and pocket it again. Nearly always this little deceit worked, and Homer would then be granted permission to do forbidden things, enter forbidden places, consult forbidden files and interview forbidden people.

But Mary was not audacious, and she would have been mortified to be caught in any sort of chicanery. Therefore she was ready. She handed a piece of paper across the desk.

"What's this?" said Doctor Rosebush.

"A court order." It had taken Mary a week. Fortunately Homer knew exactly who to talk to in the Cambridge Courthouse, and at last his friend Ernie, after questioning Mary severely, had made out the necessary document.

"I see." Doctor Rosebush read it through, and began at once to talk.

42

LEONARD WAS SPENDING THE MORNING IN MOUNT Auburn Cemetery, taking his turn at keeping watch. He had brought with him a heavy tome, *The Proceedings of the Twenty-fifth Congress of the International Union of Crystallography.*

He sat on the grass on the little bluff above the Fell family plot with the book open on his knees and tried to read. *It may be remarked that analogous cases are sometimes met with in crystal chemistry.*

The day was warm, the words blurred on the page.

Holding his place, he lay back on the grass. The Goodyear blimp was passing overhead, moving slowly in the direction of Fresh Pond.

Once again Leonard was reminded of an Escher invention, a lattice of blimplike fish going down and back forever. The blimp seemed as motionless as the fish.

A small plane was noisier. It whined across the sky, dragging a long banner with an illegible message. Leonard tried to ignore the blimp and the plane. Lying flat, he lifted the heavy book over his head. *It may be remarked that analogous cases are sometimes met with in crystal chemistry.*

Even in the dappled shade, the mid-June sun was hot. Below the looping curve of Willow Avenue he could hear the buzzing sound of a motorized trimmer shaving the grass around the mausoleums beside Auburn Lake. Another machine whizzed down Willow Avenue, its tiny front wheels backing and whirling in and out among the graves.

And someone else was coming. Leonard lifted his head. At once he was alarmed. Maybe he should warn that guy on the lawn mower not to run down the people who were climbing up from Auburn Lake and crossing Willow Avenue. But the lawn mower buzzed out of the way, and the procession moved relentlessly forward.

Leonard had seen the black-veiled woman twice before, and the mournful men with bowed heads who were carrying the small casket. He watched as they circled the Fell family plot and began to climb again, almost floating up the hill to the triangular monument of the Mountforts, then crossing the road and dropping down Oxalis Path.

When they came circling back up from Auburn Lake, Leonard was not surprised. It was merely that famous print come to life again, Escher's little men going up and down forever on their strange and ever-returning staircase.

He sat up. They were gone.

Picking up his book, Leonard got to his feet. As he walked back to the great Egyptian gate he noticed something that gave him a shock of pleasure. It was his shadow, moving in front of him across the grass, across the path, across the paved surface of Beech Avenue.

It was two-dimensional! A shadow had length and breadth but no depth at all. The leaves that had been plastered to the road by last night's rain were different. They had depth, and so did the thinnest piece of paper. But not a shadow. A shadow glided across the earth without any substance of its own. It was not a material object, it was merely the absence of something, a skim of nothingness thrown down by an obstacle blocking out the light.

And on his way home he remembered the mirrors in Frieda's abandoned apartment, and saw at once that shadows were not the only two-dimensional things in the world. Reflections in a mirror were two-dimensional as well. They did not really exist. Like shadows they were illusions.

That night he lay in bed, thinking about the blimp that had passed over his head that afternoon, floating so dreamily in the sky above the trees. What a view it must have of Boston and Cambridge and the bridges over the Charles and the thousands of cars speeding along both sides of the river. What a privilege to overlook it all, to see Old Ironsides docked at Long Wharf and the tall cranes hoisting cargoes in and out of ships.

Without any sense of transition, Leonard found himself aloft. Yes, there was the cemetery, lovely and green, spotted with white shapes like a sheep pasture, already drifting out of sight. Now the blimp was floating over the Bunker Hill monument in Charlestown and the pointed top of the obelisk was veering away to the east. Soon the suburbs spread out below him, shopping centers, neighborhoods, thousands of houses—Arlington, Belmont, Waltham, Lexington—and here was the town of Concord with its two winding rivers. And now he could see the bend where the Sudbury River opened out and turned south, and—yes, of course—there on the shore was the small house of Mary and Homer Kelly.

At the controls of his airy vessel Leonard understood at once that the Kellys' house was smack at the corner of a geometric figure. It was a simple matter of triangulation, that ancient system for determining the shape, size and curvature of the earth. *When one side and two angles of a triangle are known, the other two sides and the third angle can be determined.*

Leonard whipped the blimp around and sent it back over the city of Cambridge. For a moment it poised over the intersection where Sibley Road ran into Brattle Street. The complicated roofs and chimneys of Mrs. Winthrop's house were turning below him, and there was Mrs. Winthrop herself at a window, leaning out, looking up at him and waving.

His landlady was clearly the second point of his immensely elongated triangulation. What was the third? The third was Frieda, but where was she? Nowhere, nowhere.

He had one side of his geometric figure, but no angles, no angles at all.

Despairing, Leonard was not surprised to find the blimp transformed into one of Escher's fish—not the fat blimplike shapes in the lattice called *Depth,* but one of the flat jolly fishes that wound around and around in a double spiral in the print called *Whirlpools,* each creature with its mad eyes fixed on the tail of the fish in front, all of them spinning deeper and deeper into an infinity of smallness, a dark and dangerous whirlpool.

43

"I HIT PAYDIRT," SAID MARY. "SHE TOLD ME everything."

"She?" said Homer. "Who do you mean?"

"Doctor Rosebush. She was the actual identical specialist in high-risk pregnancy who attended Patrick's mother through eight miscarriages. She remembered everything from all those years ago. Her patient seems to have left an indelible impression."

"What sort of impression?"

Mary remembered the slight grimace that had accompanied Doctor Rosebush's cool clinical account. "Not altogether favorable."

"You mean she was the same doctor?" Homer was astonished. "From all those years ago? How old is she anyway?"

"Doctor Rosebush? Oh, I don't know. Fifty?" Mary brushed the question aside. "Listen, Homer, she told me something amazing."

"After her sixth miscarriage," said Doctor Rosebush, her words coming out in a rush, "I wanted to urge her to stop trying, to give up and adopt a baby, because suffering through failure after failure is so hard on a woman's body."

"You wanted to, but you didn't?"

"Of course not. I never tell a woman to stop trying. But I did suggest that she see a therapist, or at least join a support group. There's a really good support group for infertile women."

"What did she say to that?"

"Oh, she'd have none of it. No, no, she had to try again. It turned out to be a matter of family pride. She had to have a child to carry on her bloodline, that's what she said." The doctor made a mock-heroic gesture. "Into the distant future."

"You mean her husband's bloodline?"

"No, no. Hers, hers. She said her husband's forebears were nothing in particular." Doctor Rosebush raised her eyes to the ceiling. "Whereas hers were something

150

super-duper."

Mary smiled. "Well, what was her glorious name? I mean her maiden name? Plantagenet?"

"She didn't say. And I certainly didn't give a damn."

It was Oliphant, thought Mary, but it didn't matter, and she returned to the subject of Mrs. Edward Fell's obstetrical history. "She did at last have a successful birth, that little boy. You helped her through it?"

"Oh, she was a hard case. But after all those failures there was no choice. I made her stay in bed for nine months. Well, we'd been through the whole thing before—the blood-count check every two weeks, ultrasound once a month."

"But then it was a successful delivery? She gave birth to a healthy little boy?"

"Oh, yes. But then—" Doctor Rosebush shook her head sadly.

"I know," said Mary softly. "There was an accident. It must have been a horrible disappointment."

"Of course, but the amazing thing is, she didn't give up. She insisted on trying again. She was frightening, grim. Well, I tried the therapist idea again, but no, that wouldn't do, I mean she was just insane. How could she give up when the genealogical future of her family was at stake? Well, of course I felt sorry for her, so I said well, all right, we'll try again."

"But, my God, wasn't she getting too old by this time?"

"Apparently not. She managed to get pregnant."

"So you put her to bed again?"

"Of course." Doctor Rosebush looked tired. She flapped her hands. "But it was another failure."

"Good lord. And that was the end of everything?"

"As far as I was concerned it was the end. When I

151

discovered what she'd done, I washed my hands of her."

"What had she done?"

Doctor Rosebush shoved back her chair, stood up and went back to the window to stare blindly at the racing traffic on Route 2. "She had cosmetic surgery."

"Cosmetic—you mean a facelift?" Mary stared at the doctor's back in disbelief.

"A facelift and breast implants, the whole thing." Doctor Rosebush turned away from the window and looked angrily at Mary. "I could have strangled her. After that long history of failed pregnancies she did violence to one part of her body as though it would have no effect on something fragile and highly susceptible in another part."

"Good God."

Homer said it too, "Good God."

Mary tried to rationalize it. "The woman must have had a colossal personal vanity, a real horror of old age. Well, I must say I don't like it either." Mary thrust violent fingers into her graying hair. "But for this wretched woman the horror of getting old was totally at war with her urge to reproduce."

Homer shook his head and murmured, "Pitiful."

Mary sighed. "Well, anyway, I'll carry on. Doctor Rosebush gave me the cosmetic surgeon's name. The trouble is—"

"I know," said Homer. "You need another court order."

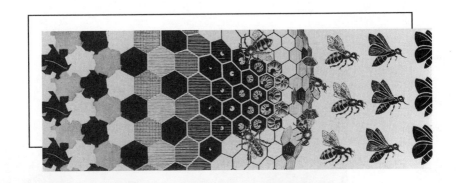

Metamorphosis

Now the rhythm changes . . .hexagons make one think of the cells in a honeycomb, and so in every cell there appears a bee larva. The fully grown larvae turn into bees which fly off into space.

M.C. Escher

44

THE COSMETIC SURGEON WAS EVEN MORE WARY THAN
Doctor Rosebush.

*Who was this woman with a court order? A
malpractice attorney? Was he being sued by a
dissatisfied patient, someone who had expected to look
more ravishing than she had ever been before?*

Doctor Faraday was a craftsman and humanitarian
whose deepest concern was with burn victims and
patients disfigured in accidents.

Many of these people had no means to pay, and
therefore he depended for most of his income on the
vanity of another kind of patient. All of the women
whose drooping faces he tightened, whose sagging
necks he reshaped, whose ugly noses he refined, whose
breasts he ballooned, whose aging romantic
expectations he revived, paid heavily for the privilege of
drinking from his fountain of youth.

On both kinds of patients he lavished the same
surgical skill and the same broad knowledge of the
latest techniques. He was adept at replacing burned
facial skin with flaps stretched up from the shoulder,
still attached to the blood supply. He could fashion an
ear, a nose or a chin with bone removed from other parts
of the body. Doctor Faraday was an artist.

He welcomed Mary courteously, but with dread.

"Doctor Faraday," said Mary, coming quickly to the
point, "I'm told that you had a patient some years ago, a
woman we're trying to find. I'm not sure we have the
right name, but I have a photograph that may show her

before her surgery." She reached in her pocketbook for the scrappy torn snapshot of the grey-haired woman standing in a doorway, but Dr. Faraday held up his hand.

"I'm sorry, but the privacy of my patients is absolute. It's the law." Then Doctor Faraday added nervously. "But I understand you have a court order?"

"Right." Mary handed it to him with an authoritative gesture, but she wasn't at all sure it would do the trick. This time the bureaucrats had given her a harder time.

"Just what, may I ask, is your interest in this matter?"

"No personal interest, I'm afraid."

"Are you in law-enforcement?"

"No, sorry."

"You mean you have not asked for the cooperation of the Cambridge Police and the Department of Missing Persons?"

"Well, no, not exactly."

But good old Jerry Neville, that wise man and legal scholar, Homer's clever friend, had suggested arguments she could repeat by rote. Mary had recited them like an automaton, and then, reluctantly, the chief bureaucrat had scrawled his signature on the new court order.

Now Doctor Faraday was satisfied. He put down the document and said softly, "What do you want to know?"

Mary handed him Leonard's fragmentary snapshot. "Do you recognize this woman?"

He looked at it for a moment and then said, "Yes." Swivelling in his chair he consulted the shelves of a bookcase, drew out a large binder and opened it on his desk. Mary watched him turn the pages. In a moment he stopped. "Here," he said, turning the book around.

"Before and after."

Mary stared, and said, "Oh, my God."

The woman in the photograph on the left was the gray-haired woman in the snapshot, haggard and hollow-eyed. The one on the right was Edward Fell's so-called niece.

45

MARY COLLECTED HER WITS. "DID SHE TELL YOU SHE was pregnant?"

"Pregnant! My God!" Dr. Faraday shot out of his chair. Sitting down again, he threw up his hands. "No, she did not. How do you know?"

"Her obstetrician told me. Dr. Rosebush."

"Doctor Rosebush? Doctor Rosalind Rosebush? But she works with high-risk patients. You don't mean—?"

"I'm afraid so."

Doctor Faraday said, "My God," again, then calmed down. "There's something else. She came back."

"She came back? You mean for more surgery?"

Doctor Faraday reached for another book, laid it on the table beside the first and turned the pages slowly. Then without a word, he turned the book around.

Mary looked back and forth between the two sets of photographs, the uncompromising records of two separate and individual transformations wrought by the surgeon's skillful knife.

The contrast in the second pair was not as dramatic as in the first. The once-rejuvenated face had sagged a little. Harsh lines had appeared between nose and mouth.

But twice-restored, it was another miracle of restored youthfulness. And yet, thought Mary, it was not a lovable face.

True, it looked young, and yet somehow old at the same time. The jawline was thinner, more bladelike. The eyes were slightly sunken in their sockets. And, therefore, it was even more like the face Mary had seen in the nursing home, the one belonging to the woman who had cooed over a visitor's baby to the horror of the senile old man she had called Uncle Edward. It was the face of the so-called niece who had rushed him out of sight. It was the face of the murdering woman who had pushed his wheelchair down the stairs.

Mary tapped the last picture. "How old is she here?"

Silently Doctor Faraday pulled open a file drawer and extracted a folder. In a moment he looked up and said, "Fifty-nine. She'd be sixty-three now."

"Amazing." Mary couldn't get over it. "She's dyed her hair, so it's no longer gray. She doesn't suffer from osteoporosis, so she stands up straight. And her voice doesn't sound cracked and old. And of course her face has been transformed. But still"—Mary put one finger on the first photograph and another on the last picture and looked up at Doctor Faraday—"isn't she physically the same? Isn't she still sixty-three years old inside?"

"Of course."

Mary made a helpless gesture. "So isn't there some way to know that she's not what she seems? I mean, if you look at it one way—forgive me—it's a devil's bargain. Doesn't the devil exact a price?"

Doctor Faraday stood up and said quietly, "Look at her hands."

158

46

AT FAIR HAVEN BAY SUMMER WAS IN ITS FULL PRIDE. The tall pines lining the ridge on the other side of the river flung out their ragged arms above a woodland in luxuriant green leaf. Fishermen put-putted past the Kellys' little dock in the direction of Lee's Bridge, where large-mouth bass were hovering. Homer and Mary sat over second cups of coffee while a tender breeze from the river fluttered the kitchen curtains.

They were trying to digest the significance of Mary's interview with Doctor Faraday.

"So she can't be the niece," said Homer, "right? She's too old to be Edward's niece."

They said it together. "She's his wife." And then Homer pounced on another obvious fact. "Patrick's mother."

"Of course!" Mary banged down her coffee cup. "She called herself Edward's niece because she had become too young and glamorous to have an old husband. It was her vanity again. But she was his wife, all right, so she's the one who writes the letters."

They stared at each other in stunned silence, and then Homer said, "Well, okay, then, who was the babysitter?"

"Well," said Mary, "it's obvious that I was wrong about the way those snapshots fitted together. The scrap with the older woman belongs with the little girl. The woman was pre-facelift, she hadn't yet been youthified. So the little girl must be her niece, Patrick's cousin. Frieda was Patrick's cousin."

Again they said it together, "The babysitter."

Mary groaned. "Oh, how awful. That means Frieda was the babysitter who walked off that night and left little Patrick all alone. So it was her fault he died. He must have toddled out of the house into the road, and then—"

Homer winced.

"Leonard won't be happy about this," said Mary.

Homer was sanctimonious. "Well, he had no business getting moony over some woman he'd only just met."

"Love at first sight," said Mary regretfully. "It's too bad it has to work out like this."

"It's his own fault." Homer shrugged. "So why do we care? We were trying to help him find his lost girlfriend, but now there's no point. She's not worth finding."

"Oh, Homer, how can you be sure? She was only a little girl then. She's grown up now."

"Tigers don't change their spots," said Homer primly.

Mary laughed. "You mean leopards. Tigers don't have spots."

Homer glared into space. "Tigers don't change their spots, leopards don't change their stripes, whales don't change their—uh—feathers."

"Oh, okay," said Mary, humoring him. "And fish don't change their—what?"

"Elbows. Fish don't change their elbows."

"Of course not, but listen, Homer, I'll bet Leonard won't lose interest in Frieda."

"Oh, well, Leonard." Homer dismissed Leonard with a wave of his hand. "Leonard sees everything through a distorting lens, those crazy prints of Escher's."

"Well, maybe his Escher lens is the truthful one, while all the rest of us are squinting at the world askew." Mary looked defiantly at Homer. "I'll bet when we find Frieda, we'll discover she's become an entirely

160

different person."

"When *you* find her, you mean. You're the one with the free time. I thought I was through with all my academic responsibilities, but I forgot about the weepers."

"Weepers?"

"Six of 'em. You know, the kids who get down on their knees to beg for a higher mark. And this afternoon I have to see a couple of parents, and you know what that'll be like. Their darling child won't be on the dean's list unless I change his grade to an A, and guess what? He's *always* been on the dean's list, he's got an affidavit in a book of gold." Homer threw up his arms and rolled his eyes at the ceiling. "And *lo,* his name led all the rest."

Mary gave in. "Well, all right, I'll carry on, but listen, Homer, you know what I think? It isn't just Frieda we're looking for. We've got to find Edward's wife. She's real, I saw her twice in the nursing home, and she's still writing those nutty letters to her dead baby. I'm convinced she killed her senile old husband, and you'll agree there's something really threatening about the video she made of the baby's grave, the one Leonard found in Frieda's coat. She's evil, Homer, that woman is truly evil."

Homer looked at his wife affectionately, thinking about something Emerson had written in his journal—*I passed him in the night.*

The same thing was happening here. Mary had passed him by. When they had first met, a long time ago, he had been the visiting scholar, the sparkling genius, while she was a humble librarian. Over the years her merit had drawn level with his, and now she was edging past him and surging ahead.

161

Not intentionally. It wasn't some kind of marital competition. Mary was younger, she was at the pinnacle of her career, while he was getting closer to retirement age and would soon be a has-been.

Gloom overcame him. He strove to hide it, trying to focus his attention on the matter in hand. "You don't suppose," he said, beginning in a slow drawl, then talking faster and ending in a sharp question—"you don't suppose the girl has disappeared because Patrick's mother killed her? What if her vengeance has already happened?"

47

THERE WAS SOMETHING UNUSUAL ABOUT MRS. Eloise Winthrop. It was true that she was a foolish old woman, a little scatterbrained in her old age, and it was also a fact that she had never been quick-witted. But there was about her an unconscious serenity, an appealing air of truthfulness and simplicity.

In these late June days of mixed weather—cold, hot, cloudy, fair—Eloise took up her post almost every day and looked down from her hilltop perch on Willow Avenue at the ongoing drama taking place below her on Narcissus Path.

In spirit she fluttered between the world of the living and the world of the dead. Thus she was a participant as well as a witness in the progression of macabre events in this green corner of the cemetery.

Around her spun the actors, the acts, the scenery and the mounting melodrama. As the gentle center of the spinning pageant, Eloise was indeed a little scatterbrained, but the needle of her compass never wavered.

This morning she wandered among Zach's neighbors on Narcissus Path, moving sympathetically from stone to stone, reading the inscriptions, pleased with the obelisk to Mary Almira Prescott Smith and the other Prescotts, fascinated by the great blocky monument devoted to the Ponds, delighted with the little Gothic temple dedicated to the memory of Nathan Appleton, enchanted by the poem inscribed on the massive central stone of the Hill family—

> *There is no death!*
> *What seems so is transition*
> *This life of mortal breath*
> *Is but a suburb of the life Elysian,*
> *Whose portal we call death.*

Oh, yes, it was so true! One crossed the bridge and entered that solemn portal, coming out on the other side into the life Elysian, which was a "suburb"—*so quaint*—of heaven.

But when she saw someone approaching the plot where little Patrick was buried, she paused to watch. It was probably little Patrick's mother. This time Eloise would speak to her and offer sympathy.

But it was not the mother, it was someone else entirely.

Frieda laid her supermarket roses on Uncle Edward's grave and stood back. For a moment she gazed down at the mounded earth, ashamed of feeling so little. Then, steeling herself, she turned to look at the small stone with the dread inscription—

PATRICK
1990–1991

Plenty of feeling now! A sob rose in Frieda's throat. With a wrench, she made herself turn away, then started in surprise.

She was looking straight into the eyes of a little old woman.

"Oh," she said, "you frightened me."

48

LEONARD MET MRS. WINTHROP ON HER WAY OUT OF the house next morning.

"Oh, good morning, Mr. Sheldrake," she said, beaming. "Such a surprise!" Then, flustered, she blushed and said, "I mean, you don't usually go out so early." She touched his arm. "Oh, forgive me. I'm such a silly old woman."

"Please call me Leonard. And I don't go out early because I work at home." Impulsively he added, "But you go for a walk every single morning, don't you, Mrs. Winthrop? That's really so admirable." *I mean, for a woman of your age.*

"Oh, yes, Leonard. You see, I go to visit Zach."

"Zach?"

Mrs. Winthrop lifted her hands to her face in consternation. "Oh, Leonard, you'll think—" She tittered, struggling for the right expression. Then, remembering a word from her youth, she said, "You'll think I'm a gaga old lady. Zach was my husband,

164

Zachariah Winthrop. He was a distinguished professor with *ten* honorary degrees. I visit him every day." Her expression changed. "That is, almost every day. Sometimes I'm too lazy." She giggled. "I just lie on the sofa."

"Oh, Mrs. Winthrop, everybody knows about your husband. Zachariah Winthrop was a famous anthropologist. You showed me his picture, the one with the Zulu tribesmen. I see, you mean, you visit his grave." Leonard shook his head in wonder.

"Of course. It's very near, right there on Willow Path."

"Willow Path? You mean in Mount Auburn Cemetery? But, Mrs. Winthrop, that's amazing. I was there just the other day. There's a triangular monument on Willow Path. You see, I'm interested in the fundamental shapes of solid geometry, crystal formations and so on. I like to find—"

"Oh," said Mrs. Winthrop, "you mean the triangular monument to the Mountforts. Of course. Do you know, I have a joke about the Mountforts? I told it to another gentleman just the other day. He was so amused." She broke off and smiled at Leonard, and there was in her smile such loving kindness that he banished all thoughts of battiness and senility. "And I've seen you there, Leonard, down there on Narcissus Path, just below Zach's neighborhood. I've seen you visiting little Patrick's grave."

He was stunned. "Patrick's grave? You mean the baby? Patrick Fell?"

"Yes, of course. And his mother, Mrs. Fell, she comes too, so often. Sometimes she takes a nap there, stretched out on the mossy grass. Such grief! After twelve long years she still visits her baby boy."

"Mrs. Winthrop." Eagerly Leonard took her hands. "Before your walk, won't you come upstairs for a cup of coffee? And I think I have a few crackers or something. Well, no, perhaps I don't."

Mrs. Winthrop didn't care. She was charmed. The barrier between tenant and landlady had broken down at last.

49

LEONARD HAD FORGOTTEN THE BUCKET. OUTDOORS the weather was sunny and warm, but it had rained in the night. The downpour had stopped, but there was still an occasional drip into the bucket from the cracked place in the ceiling, *plink-plonk.*

Mrs. Winthrop saw the bucket at once and said, "Gracious me!" She turned to Leonard in distress. "The roof, oh, Leonard, you told me about the roof. I'll call someone at once."

"Oh, that's okay," said Leonard. "It hasn't been any trouble." Glancing around, he wished he had made his bed. Hastily he yanked the spread over his disordered sheets.

He need not have bothered. Mrs. Winthrop liked the manly messiness of his apartment. Leonard was a young male, after all, and messiness was the masculine way. She had always enjoyed the strong virile habits of healthy young men.

She remembered with a tender sigh the pungent aroma that had so often hung around Zach when he needed a bath. And in bed he had been a mastering tiger.

166

People sometimes pretended that men and women were not really very different, but of course they were. Men were powerful and strong, women soft and sweet. She, Eloise, had always depended on the wise authority of her husband—

Auto mechanic: "Mrs. Winthrop, what's wrong with your car?"

"Oh, I'm sorry. I just don't understand a single thing about automobiles. You'll have to ask my husband."

Plumber: "Your husband called me, Mrs. Winthrop? What's the problem?"

"Oh, dear, I think it's something to do with the furnace, but you'll have to speak to Professor Winthrop."

Certified public accountant: "Mrs. Winthrop, I have a few questions about your tax return."

"Oh, I'm so sorry, Mr. Pratt, I just don't understand financial matters at all. You'll have to speak to Zachariah."

Zachariah: "Eloise, I've got such a heavy load of work. Don't you think you could pay the bills this month, just this once?"

"Oh, Zach, dear, you know what a silly woman I am. I just don't know anything about checks and bills and those other things—what are they called? Stubs? Well, never mind, dear. I'll bring you a cup of cocoa and sit right here beside you."

Since her husband's death Mrs. Winthrop was even more unable to cope. Four or five times a year she brought a bag of puzzling communications to the office of her accountant in Harvard Square. All the envelopes were unopened, including a number of boring-looking ones from someone called Schwab.

Leonard urged her to sit down in his only comfortable

167

chair. He plugged in his electric kettle and heated water for the teabag. At last he sat down on the end of his bed and said, "Mrs. Winthrop, I should explain. I'm interested in that baby's grave. There's someone I'm trying to find. I think she's a member of that family."

Leonard did not pass on to Mrs. Winthrop the ugly information about Frieda that Mary had told him on the phone. She had explained it gently, knowing he would be upset to learn that Frieda had been the babysitter on that sad day twelve years ago. Leonard wasn't sure he believed it anyway.

Now he hitched his chair forward. "Would you tell me, Mrs. Winthrop, what you see down there on Narcissus Path? You say you've seen the baby's mother?"

"Well, of course, I don't know for sure that she's his mother. But who else would care so much? And she was there when they buried someone else."

"Edward? You mean Edward Fell? You saw him being buried?"

"Oh, yes. It was rather sad. There were so few flowers, so few people in attendance. But another relative brought flowers just yesterday. A few roses for her uncle, rather ordinary, but of course it's the thought that counts."

"Who brought flowers? Who was it, Mrs. Winthrop? Did you see the person?"

"Oh, yes. It was a young woman in dungarees. Her light hair was cut very short."

"Frieda," whispered Leonard. "It was Frieda."

"Who?" said Mrs. Winthrop. But she was thinking of something else. "Oh, Leonard dear, have you seen the peacock?"

"The peacock? What peacock?"

"There's a peacock. I've seen it several times. How I

wish it would spread its tail!"

"The woman in blue jeans, Mrs. Winthrop. Did she stay long?"

Mrs. Winthrop gazed vaguely at the mysterious electronic equipment on Leonard's desk. "She was trying not to cry. So right away I knew what to do. I took her hand and led her up to Willow Avenue, to our own special neighborhood. Oh, Leonard, you should see how nice it is there. I've made quite a little camp, a home away from home. Of course one has to be careful, because the Mount Auburn people don't like you to leave things beside the graves. You know, dear—teddy bears, china angels, little statues of St. Francis."

"People leave things?"

"Oh, my, yes. So I've found a place in the bushes, and I tuck my things out of sight."

"What sort of things, Mrs. Winthrop?

She smiled, wishing he would call her by her first name. After all, he had asked her to call him Leonard. But she knew it would make him uncomfortable to call her Eloise.

"Well, let me see. A tin of cookies, for one thing. I like to offer refreshments to people passing by. And I have a small blanket in a plastic bag. And—oh! There's something new, cracked corn! Can you guess what it's for?"

Leonard was willing to be patient forever. "For the peacock?"

"Oh, yes, the peacock. I wish he'd come back. I've seen him twice." Mrs. Winthrop sipped her coffee, then returned to the subject of the young woman at Patrick's grave. "We settled down side by side next to Zach and I brought out my tin of cookies. But first she jumped up, all excited, because she could see the tower."

"The tower?"

"The tower on the top of the hill. And then she said something so funny. She said it was like a piece in a game. A chess game, I think." Mrs. Winthrop frowned. "Unless it was checkers? Anyway, pretty soon I asked her to come home with me because she began to cry."

"You brought her home? You mean she was here, she was right here?"

"Oh, yes. She was really pleased, I could tell. She liked all of Zach's things in the hall. You know, the totem pole and the hookah. She really liked the hookah."

Leonard waited, his mind in a tumult.

"And then she told me why she had been crying. She said her mother and father had been killed in a plane crash a long time ago. You remember, Leonard? That terrible plane crash in Ireland? Or was it Canada?" Mrs. Winthrop looked confused. "Well, it doesn't matter. She went on to tell me that the sudden loss of her parents wasn't the only terrible thing. There had been something else, just the day before. Something so terrible, she couldn't talk about it. She just sobbed and sobbed. I put my arms around her, and after awhile she stopped crying and we had tea."

"She didn't say what the terrible thing was?"

"No." Mrs. Winthrop rose shakily to her feet. "Thank you, Leonard dear. You must be so busy. I'll go now."

He was disappointed. "Did she tell you where she lives? Do you know her last name?"

"Oh, no." Mrs. Winthrop walked to the door, moving a little stiffly. "But she did say one more thing. I didn't understand it at all."

"What did she say, Mrs. Winthrop?" Leonard jumped up and opened the door to the stairs.

She beamed at him and started down the long flight. But at the first landing she stopped. Her rosy smiling face looked up at him and her voice floated up the stairs.

"She said, '*No child of my own.*'"

50

AND THAT AFTERNOON THE POSTAL SERVICE TO THE Other Side delivered another letter. Leonard found it in the metal box behind Patrick's small headstone.

He had come in the wild hope that Frieda might come back. But now he cursed himself for missing Patrick's mother, the madwoman who wrote the letters. She had been here, she had opened the box and dropped the letter in.

Leonard lifted it out with trembling hands, slipped it out of its envelope and held it up in the grey light. It fluttered in his hands and nearly blew away.

Oh, my darling child, I'm so tired. So tired of half-measures. So tired of the burden I've been carrying so long. So tired of the injustice! Your father was such a mollycoddle, such a stumbling block. Somehow I couldn't bring myself to act while he was alive. But now that he's gone, I can set things right. Justice, justice!

Your loving Mother

❋

Leonard thundered up the porch steps and banged on the door.

The answer came from behind him, a shout from the river. "Leonard, ahoy."

Homer Kelly was maneuvering a canoe into the

171

shallows. Leonard ran down the steps and helped him haul it up on the muddy shore.

"I tried to phone you," he said, shouldering one of the paddles.

"Sorry." Homer waved the other paddle at the river. "I've been out there all morning. Hey, you know what? I saw three great blue herons. How's that for a morning's work?"

Homer's voice was a little hollow, because his wife's work that morning was so much more important—except of course, as Homer kept telling himself, when considered on the scale of absolute value, where great blue herons were somewhere near the top.

Mary was moderating a panel of important scholars at the Schlesinger Library. Five learned feminists were at this moment addressing a large audience, discussing issues of gender, virtual sexuality and spiritual marriage in the poetry of Emily Dickinson. Homer felt left out.

"Here," he said, taking Leonard's paddle, "they go under the porch."

Leonard followed him up the steps. "It's another of those kooky letters. Really scary this time."

"No kidding? That explains why your forehead's all wrinkled with care." Homer gestured at a chair. "Sit down." He sat down himself and pulled off his muddy shoes.

Leonard took from his pocket the strange new letter from Patrick's grave and silently handed it over.

Homer read it, then jumped to his feet. "Coffee, Leonard? I can't handle this without a cup of coffee." From the kitchen he yelled back, "What does she mean by half-measures?" There were rattles and bangs. "And, Christ, there it is again, the word justice. What does she mean? Sugar, Leonard? Milk?" Homer flung open the

172

refrigerator door. "Oh, sorry, no milk." He came back with the two mugs of coffee and handed one to Leonard. "Hey, why don't you sit down?"

Leonard would not sit down. He stood nervously in the middle of the room, gesticulating with his cup. "Mary told me the baby's death was Frieda's fault, remember? She said Frieda was the babysitter." Coffee slopped from the mug.

"Whoopsie," said Homer, "no problem." He bounced into the kitchen, bounced back, dropped to his knees and swabbed at the floor. "Right, Frieda was the babysitting cousin. So, of course by justice the letter must mean the mother of the baby wants revenge on the cousin." Homer stood up and looked gravely at Leonard. "Who just happens to be her niece Frieda, the babysitter responsible for the baby's death."

"Homer, it was a long time ago. She was only a child." More coffee slopped over the rim of Leonard's cup. At once he snatched Homer's dishcloth, dropped to his knees and swiped at the floor.

"Wait a sec, you missed some." Homer got down again too, grabbed the cloth and groveled under the table.

There were thumps on the stairs and Mary Kelly threw open the door. At the sight of two dignified doctors of philosophy crawling on the floor she burst out laughing, dumped her briefcase on a chair and dropped on hands and knees. "Oh, goody, let's play bears."

"It's all his fault," said Homer cheerfully, getting up. "Poor guy's all thumbs."

"I'm afraid he's right," said Leonard dolefully, helping Mary to her feet. "I'm sorry."

"Coffee, dearheart?" said Homer. "That is, if there's

173

any coffee left. If your oafish guest hasn't thrown it all over the place." Again he shouted from the kitchen. "How was the panel? Did you ladies get through the whole thing without pulling each other's hair?"

"Oh, shut up, Homer." Mary grinned at Leonard as Homer handed her a cup. "Well, of course there were a few scratched faces. That woman from Swarthmore had really sharp fingernails."

They settled down. Leonard picked up the magazines on the coffee table and patted them into a cube. Homer handed Mary the strange new letter from the box behind Patrick's little headstone. She read it and murmured. "Oh, my God."

Leonard put the magazines down precisely in the middle of the table and related his conversation with Mrs. Winthrop. "She's my landlady. She saw Frieda at Patrick's grave."

"Your landlady!"

"Yes, Mrs. Winthrop visits her husband's grave in Mount Auburn nearly every day. It's on Willow Avenue."

Homer smote his forehead. "But I've seen her. Mrs. Winthrop's your landlady? Mrs. Zachariah Winthrop? Widow of the great anthropologist?"

"Yes, of course." Leonard was startled. "You've seen her? Where?"

"Right there on Willow Avenue in the cemetery. It was the day Mary forced me to carry on my important scholarly research on a collapsing stool, waiting for Patrick's mother to post another letter. Of course she didn't show, so it was a waste of time."

Leonard leaned forward eagerly. "Did you talk to her? Mrs. Winthrop?"

"Oh, she was charming. She took me on a tour of all

174

the dead folks in the neighborhood. She told me her mother was invited to a garden party by Isabella Stewart Gardner. Hey, Leonard, you know what kind of sandwiches they had at the garden party? You'd be interested in Mrs. Gardner's sandwiches, Leonard. Teeny triangles, that's what they were. Basic universal shape, right? Undergirding the universe?" Homer gazed seraphically at the ceiling. "I'm really fond of things that undergird the universe. Or overarch it. Overarching the universe, that's nice too."

Mary poked him and turned to Leonard. "Did I hear you correctly? Did you say that Mrs. Winthrop actually saw Frieda?"

Leonard smiled faintly. "She told me all about it. Frieda was putting flowers on Edward's grave. She's such an old dear, my landlady. She said hello to Frieda and pretty soon Frieda was crying on her shoulder and telling her about a terrible time when she was a child. Her parents were killed in that famous plane crash off Nova Scotia. Remember that big 747 that went down in the north Atlantic? I looked it up. It was 1991."

"The year of Patrick's death," murmured Mary.

"Right, and then Frieda told Mrs. Winthrop that something also happened the day before, something so awful she couldn't talk about it. And of course it must have been—" Leonard's face changed, his eyes watered, he stared stupidly into space, sucked in his breath and sneezed. Recovering, he pawed at his pocket. Mary handed him a box of tissues and he disappeared behind a cloud.

It was obvious to Homer that Leonard's sneeze was a physical response to mental anguish. Brutally he finished the sentence. "It must have been the baby's death, which was her own damned fault."

"Oh, God," whispered Leonard, coming into view again.

"Well, okay, okay," said Mary. "The point is, we've got to get going. We can't just moon around in the cemetery hoping somebody will show up. Did your landlady find out where Frieda lives?"

In the tower of Babel, thought Leonard, *in the chessboard town, in the mill beside the waterfall.* He shook his head. "She didn't even ask her name."

"Well, then, how do you know it was Frieda?"

"She described her. I knew it was Frieda."

"Well, look here, Leonard," began Homer, "that damned girl—" Mary kicked him, and he went on apologetically, "I mean that poor girl Frieda, she's in real trouble. That insane aunt of hers, the baby's deranged mother, wants to punish her for Patrick's death. God knows what she'll do."

In her long professional career Mary had become accustomed to chairing meetings. She could handle the self-indulgent talker, the obstructionist, the muddled introducer of side-issues, the rambling storyteller. And she knew precisely when the moment for decision had arrived. In this three-person conference it was time to gavel the participants to order.

"Well, then," she said, "what's our first objective? We want to find Frieda, we want to find her aunt. So far we've had no luck with their current addresses. Oh, of course I asked Doctor Rosebush, the obstetrician, and also Doctor Faraday, the cosmetic surgeon. All they had for Mrs. Fell was a post office box number in Watertown, the same one they have in the nursing home."

"Probably her personal post office box to the other world," growled Homer sarcastically. "Well, did you

176

follow it up?"

Mary glanced at Leonard. "He did."

"Right," said Leonard. "I went to the central post office in Watertown and asked who was paying for Box 321. At first they refused to tell me." He shrugged. "Well, of course they have to be careful. How do they know somebody isn't a wife beater or some kind of dangerous stalker?"

"At first?" repeated Homer. "You mean they relented?"

Leonard smiled wanly and reached out to the Kellys' coffee table. Some of the magazines had slipped sideways. "Oh, it was so innocuous, they saw it couldn't do any harm. The box was reassigned just last week. The Girl Scouts have it now. It's a box number for the Girl Scouts of America."

Homer laughed and slapped his knee.

"Meeting adjourned," said Mary.

51

MARY HAD TWO REASONS FOR VISITING THE ABERDEEN Street Nursing Home.

One was to see her old friend Barbara, who had been neglected during the tumultuous inpouring of final exams and the writing of her important speech. Now that her talk was ready and her academic duties done, there was time for the duties of friendship.

The other reason was her decision to make another assault on the nursing home records. Surely the death of one of its residents, Edward Fell, would have called for all kinds of documentation, death certificates, invoices and bills addressed to the party responsible for the cost of his care? In the Aberdeen Street Nursing Home she would at last ferret out the whereabouts of Patrick's dangerous mother.

Barbara smiled radiantly and reached out her arms as Mary came in. Barbara's arthritic hands were cramped and gnarled, but her eyes were clear and her speech was quick. "I should have called you," she said. "Something's happened."

"Let's go to your room," said Mary, whisking Barbara's wheelchair away from the feeble old men and women lined up in a row, gently waiting to blur out of life.

In Barbara's corridor her roommate Jenny stopped the wheelchair's progress and buttonholed Mary. "I know what you're thinking," she said craftily. "You think I like you. Well, I don't."

"That's all right, Jenny," said Mary, smiling at her. "I like you, anyway."

Jenny glowered and said, "That's a lie." Then as Mary swooped Barbara's wheelchair through the open door of her room they could hear Jenny accosting Dorothy, the head nurse. "You think I like you, but I don't. And what's more, I never did and I never will."

In the glare of the overhead fluorescent light, Barbara's face was greenish-gray. "Pass me that bottle of pills," she said. "It's too soon for the next one, but the hell with it."

"Right," said Mary, reaching for the bottle. "The hell with it." She extracted a pill and handed Barbara a glass of water.

Barbara swallowed, handed back the glass, leaned back with closed eyes, and explained about Jenny. "Her husband was a preacher with a big congregation of

178

hellfire Methodists. Terrible thing, being a clergyman's wife. I suppose Jenny had to be sweet, and nothing but sweet, to a thousand people for years and years. Now, glory be, she's free at last."

Mary sat down on the bed, murmured, "Free at last," and waited.

In a moment Barbara opened her eyes and pulled herself upright. "I said I should have called you."

"Yes, Barbara. What about?"

The fluorescent lights flickered and buzzed. "There was a ceremony," said Barbara solemnly. "We were all invited. Presentation of a big check by Edward's niece."

"Edward's niece! She's not his niece."

"Well, whatever. Miz Whooseywhatsis had this big cardboard check for a hundred thousand dollars. She handed it to Dorothy, and we were all supposed to clap. I didn't."

"Blood money," said Mary, leaning forward eagerly.

Barbara nodded. "A bribe to shut Dorothy up. Well, I don't think Dorothy would have accused the woman of shoving Edward down the stairs, but Whooseywhatsis didn't want to take a chance."

"Do you think she made a bargain?"

"You mean with Dorothy? Hell, no. But poor Dorothy, she wasn't about to turn down a check for a hundred thousand dollars. Think what it would buy! A few motorized wheelchairs—I could use one myself—and more help. The practical nurses are run off their feet, getting everybody up, bathing and dressing all of us, changing the sheets. No, no, she couldn't turn it down. So she had to smile and accept that big bragging piece of cardboard and say"—Barbara grimaced—"Oh, how terribly nice of you! We're all so terribly grateful!"

Mary wanted to say, "Oh, God, yes, Barbara. You

should have called me," but she didn't.

She stayed for an hour while they talked comfortably about their old friends, Mary's students, the mess in Washington. The latter was Barbara's profoundest interest. She was an ardent revolutionary who could deliver a hilarious version of the anarchist theme song, "It's Auntie Olga's Turn to Throw the Bomb."

But when Jenny came back and threw her arms around Mary and cried, "You don't like me, do you?" it was time to say goodbye. Mary hugged Jenny and kissed Barbara, then walked down the corridor to talk to the head nurse.

"Oh, she's such an awful woman," said Dorothy, "that Eleanor Fell. Thank the lord, I never have to see her again. It was god-awful, the way she was always taking me aside and whispering things."

"Whispering things? What sort of things?"

There was a pause while Dorothy took on the persona of Edward's so-called niece. Her eyes widened. Staring fiercely at Mary she whispered, *"My uncle's psychiatrist diagnosed his manic-depressive disorder and senile dementia. He advised me"*—Dorothy's whisper became a hiss—*"to seek power of attorney."*

"Power of attorney?" Mary shook her head in pity. "Oh, poor Edward."

Dorothy sighed and changed the subject. "You asked for her address and I told you we only had a box number. But then I looked way back, because I remembered that a certain Mrs. Fell had put her old mother in here once, a long time ago." She opened a large notebook. "The old mother was a Mrs. Oliphant. She was not very happy here, and she didn't last long. Half a minute, she's in here somewhere."

"Oliphant?" repeated Mary softly.

Dorothy flipped the pages. "Yes, here we are. In those days Mrs. Edward Fell lived in Cambridge at 147 Gideon Street. She probably isn't there any more."

"Probably not, but thank you so much," said Mary fervently, writing it down.

Out-of-doors, she was halfway to her car when she wheeled around and went back inside.

Dorothy was sorting her files. She looked up in surprise.

"One more question," said Mary. "How old do you think she is, this Eleanor Fell?"

"Oh"—Dorothy gazed out the window, considering—"in her mid-forties?"

"What about her hands? Did you ever notice her hands?"

"Her hands?" Dorothy looked open-mouthed at Mary.

Mary told Homer about it later. "The way she looked at me, Homer, you would have recognized the look of wild surmise. You know, the one in the poem, the way stout Cortez stared at the Pacific."

Homer guffawed. "Oh, right. This here continent ain't Cathay. There's a whole goddamn ocean between us and Cathay." He calmed down. "What did she say?"

"She said she'd noticed it especially when Edward's so-called niece handed over that big cardboard check. Her hands were knotted with blue veins. They were the hands of an old woman."

52

GIDEON STREET IN CAMBRIDGE—MARY FOUND IT ON the map, tapped her finger on the spot and said, "Come with me, Homer."

"Heck, no." Homer shook his head sadly. "It wouldn't work. I've tried that trick once too often, pretending to be back at my childhood home." Clasping his hands, he whined, "Oh, the dear old place where I lived as a boy! Oh, please, dear lady, may I see it once more before I die?"

Mary laughed. "Last time, as I recall, a couple of drug dealers threw you out. But, Homer dear, this neighborhood won't be like that. It's pretty respectable."

"That's why it's so right for you. Females and houses, they go together."

Mary opened her mouth to protest, but Homer was off and away, building a tower of piffle. "It's the nesting instinct, that's what it is, a sex-linked gene on the chromosome chain. Mary, dear, you know perfectly well the way the mama bird behaves, lining her nest with feathers and bits of string and ten thousand square feet of oak flooring and a marble foyer and a step-down living room. All that domestic kind of thing."

Mary laughed in spite of herself. "Oh, Homer, you know perfectly well I'm not like that."

"Oh, no? What about that mirror you brought back from Venice? Gold cherubs and curlicues all over?"

"Oh, right." Mary had to confess defeat. The Venetian mirror was the darling of her heart, but Homer had complained that it wouldn't go with the cattails in the river or the Canada geese flying over the roof or the map of Fair Haven Bay on the wall. In fact he had been right. It had looked so out of place that she had hung it in the basement, where it gave her a jolt of happiness whenever she descended the stairs. There it was, that elegant souvenir from the city of Venice, enshrining within its glittering frame the underwear on the clothes rack and her own tall shape as she folded the laundry.

So she went by herself.

Gideon Street was pretty much what she had expected, a tree-lined road with Victorian houses alternating with newer ones. Obviously the owners of the old places had sold off their side lots. When?

The newer ones were vaguely colonial. Some were ranch houses with picture windows. Built in the 1950s, guessed Mary, paid for with interest-free mortgages from the G.I. bill.

Number 147 was newer. It was a split-level with an entrance halfway between the first and second floors and a big garage at one side. A couple of pretentious one-and-a-half-story columns flanked the cement steps to the front door.

Mary stared at the door. Was it the one in Leonard's snapshots? It was an ordinary standard-looking door. She couldn't be sure.

Boldly, Mary pushed the bell. At once a boy jerked the door open and stared at her. A vacuum cleaner droned upstairs.

"Hi, there," said Mary. "Is your mother at home? My name's Mary Kelly."

The boy turned his head and hollered, "Hey, Mom."

The musical pitch of the vacuum whined down from a screaming high note to a growl to silence. A woman's

183

voice shrilled, "Is it a salesperson?"

Mary leaned forward and called, "I just want to ask about some people who lived here twelve years ago."

The boy shrugged and thumped downstairs. A pink face surrounded with pin curls appeared over the upper railing. "Sorry, can't help you. We only been here, like, two years."

"Well, can you tell me the name of previous owners?"

"Jordan, family named Jordan, but they'd only been here six months. I mean she told me, her husband got this job in Georgia so they had to move south and she was really pissed."

Mary leaned farther into the doorway and craned her neck. "Well, do you know who lived here before that?"

"Nope. Sorry." The face disappeared and once again the vacuum shrilled into noisy life.

"Well, thank you anyway," bawled Mary.

"Don't mention it," screeched the present owner of 147 Gideon Street.

Mary walked back to the sidewalk. What about the neighbors? Perhaps one of them would remember the people who lived at Number 147 twelve years ago. Surely they would remember the horrible night when the baby was killed.

The next house was a gambrel colonial with chunky pendants under the overhang. A woman answered the door, swinging it wide, beaming at Mary. Then her face fell. Turning, she called to the next room, "It's not Joan."

There was a summons, "Come on, Phyllis, it's your bid."

Phyllis stared at Mary and said coldly, "May I help you?"

184

Mary talked fast. "I wonder if you can tell me who was living next door twelve years ago? I'm trying to find the family—"

She stopped as the lady of the house shook her head, pulled down her girdle with a jerk and closed the door to a narrow crack. "Sorry, I can't help you," she said, one eye and three teeth visible for a second. "We just moved here from Arlington."

So that was that. There were five other houses on this side of the street, but at three of them no one answered the doorbell and at the other two the answer was disappointing. Neither family had lived in the neighborhood more than six years. No one remembered the Fells.

But at the house directly across from Number 147 Mary seemed to be on the right track.

"Twelve years? Funny, that's exactly how long we been here, us Swansons."

"Then you must have known the family across the street?"

"No, we never met. I think they moved away soon after we came." The man giggled. "Buncha tramps today, everybody in the modern world."

"Well, do you remember the accident that happened here, right here on this street, on the night of May twenty-ninth?"

Swanson was a chuckler. "What a coincidence. Musta been the night before we moved in on Memorial Day. A baby, right? Babysitter's fault, baby got killed? Sure, we heard about it, but it happened just before we got here, just before the moving van arrived with all our stuff. Nice neighbor. Miz Brisket, dead now, she come over with a coffeecake, told us all about it."

Mary hated to give up. "Well, do you know the name

185

of the previous owner of your house?"

"Not an owner, this place is just a rental." Mr. Swanson cackled joyfully. "No, I remember the name of the people rented before us, is all. Dunphy, name of Dunphy. Had to leave in a hurry. There was some kind of family trouble, divorce maybe, that's why they left. Or maybe it was legal hot water. Miz Brisket, she give us the lowdown on the whole neighborhood." Mr. Swanson cackled again, rejoicing in human frailty. "Told us the dirt about everybody—who beat his wife, whose little kid was a shoplifter."

"You say the Dunphys were in some kind of legal trouble? She told you that?"

"Could be. Somebody was. I forget who."

Mary poised her pen over her notebook. "Mr. Swanson, do you know where they went?"

"Who, Mr. and Mrs. Dunphy?" Swanson shook his head, grinning, enjoying his role as the bearer of bad news, the prophet of gloom. "Nope. Haven't a clue."

"Well, the owner of the house, then," urged Mary. "May I have their name and phone number?"

Mr. Swanson's chuckles were growing tiresome. "Oh, there's a different one now. The old owner, she died too. Grim reaper been busy. He's got this big scythe. You know how it is. He never stops bringing in the sheaves."

53

THIS TIME IT WAS UP TO HOMER. HE LISTENED SOBERLY as Mary told him about her unsatisfactory exploration of Gideon Street.

"That's all you've got? Dunphy? The name of the people who lived across the street at the time?"

"Yes, but listen to this, Homer. They moved out of the house the very same night."

A fly droned around the room, buzzing low over their spinach soup, threatening to come down on the edge of a bowl. Homer jumped up and snatched the flyswatter. "The same night? You mean the same night the baby was killed on the road?"

"Right. And they were in a tearing hurry to move out, that's what Mr. Swanson said."

The fly drifted to the counter, interesting itself in a box of blueberries. Homer brandished the flyswatter and it dodged sideways, coming down on a china teapot. "Who's Mr. Swanson?"

"He lives there now, in the house across the street. He said the reason the Dunphys were in such a hurry was, maybe they were in trouble with the law."

"Maybe?"

"Well, it was some reason or other, like a divorce or some other sort of family disagreement. He told me somebody in the neighborhood had been in legal hot water, and it might have been the Dunphys, he wasn't exactly sure."

The fly rose from the teapot. Homer made a wild swipe and missed. "What you need is a street list. The city of Cambridge, they'll have a list of all the residents on every street. There's a new list every year. If you get hold of the one for the right year, you'll find the Dunphys. So at least you'd get their full names, and then you'd have something to work with."

"And the legal problem? Wouldn't it be on a computer somewhere? Couldn't you look up a name, and if they've got a record, it'll be there?"

"Right," whispered Homer. "Wait a sec." The fly was circling over the sideboard, buzzing lower and lower, aiming for a pile of papers. Homer waited for the six-point landing, lifted the swatter high and whammed it down. The fly disappeared, leaving a smear on a page of scholarly footnotes.

"Oh, bravo," said Mary. "Come on, Homer, sit down and eat your soup."

Homer hung the swatter back on its nail. "You get me the full names of those people, and I'll do the rest."

"What about the issue of privacy? Isn't it illegal to give out that kind of information? I hope you won't need another court order?"

"Oh, no. Don't forget my excellent friend Ernest McAllister. Tried and true-blue, that's my Ernie."

54

TWELVE YEARS IS A LONG TIME IN THE LIFE OF A bureaucracy. Most of the men and women who had been functionaries, twelve years back, in the Middlesex County Criminal Records Department had been replaced by new civil servants.

The ex-county clerk who had served the subpoena on

Jack Dunphy on the morning of May 29, 1991, now lived far away. He was the candlepin bowling champion of Daytona Beach, Florida. Thus he seldom thought of the old days, being too taken up with intricacies of footwork, grip, stance and follow-through to reminisce about the bad old days of rain, snow, and the dangerous rage of the people on whom he had served his subpoenas.

Therefore no one was left who remembered the time when the Dunphys had disappeared, way back in 1991. The frustration of the county clerk and the obscenities of the prosecuting attorney were all forgotten. The case was merely cold print on page 778a of the county archives, cross-referenced to file 19,456B in the federal records office.

It had been a case of simple tax fraud. Jack Dunphy had failed to list on his federal tax return for the previous year the sum of five-hundred-thousand dollars of questionable income. Lawyers for the Internal Revenue Service were curious to know (a) the source of the money and (b) why it had not been itemized on his federal return.

Before dawn on May 30, 1991, Jack and Lexine Dunphy had fled their rented house at 142 Gideon Street. Jack had never been seen again.

But Homer found Lexine. She was in the telephone book for the western suburbs.

Consulting the phone book had been Mary's idea. Granted, it was a stupid idea, but she had been feeling pretty stupid that day. Her summer conference was over. She had delivered her keynote address. At last, emotionally exhausted, she was stretched out on a lawn chair on the porch, staring blankly at Fair Haven Bay and thinking idly about the Dunphys, when it occurred to her that she could still handle the alphabet. Strolling indoors, she stared at the pile of telephone books.

There were fifteen Dunphys. One was Lexine. She lived in Arlington.

"Of course she may not be the right Lexine," cautioned Homer.

"But Lexine's not exactly a common name. Especially when combined with Dunphy. I'll bet she's the same one."

Homer's appetite was whetted by his disappointment in the Criminal Records Department. He slapped the page and said, "I'll go."

Lexine Dunphy's house was a modest ranch in a neighborhood of similar houses. The lawn was uncut, there were flagstones missing from the walk, the shades were drawn.

"Good morning," said Homer politely, when a grossly obese woman opened the door. "My name is Homer Kelly. I'm trying to learn something about one of your neighbors on Gideon Street in Cambridge twelve years ago. I hope I'm speaking to the right person? Mrs. Lexine Dunphy?"

Lexine gaped at Homer, then invited him in. He suspected she would have welcomed in the paper boy.

In the kitchen Lexine removed the dirty dishes from the table and piled them with a heap of others in the sink. She swabbed feebly at the oilcloth and said, "Sit down."

Homer pitied the large unkempt woman in the grubby kitchen.

"You know what today is?" said Lexine, thumping herself down. "It's my fifteenth wedding anniversary." The announcement was sarcastic.

Homer gave up any thought of asking questions. It was time to listen. Lexine was letting it all hang out. As she talked, he translated, changing half-truths into candid confessions, changes of expression into revelations.

Her marital history was clear. Homer itemized it in his head—

1. *Honeymoon over, Lexine gains weight, Jack's belly swells.*

2. *Domesticity turns slovenly.*

3. *Moments of togetherness reduced to television, Budweiser, salty snacks, greasy chins, fat bodies slumped in big soft chairs.*

4. *Cute girl at the office! Jack perks up, slims down, buys flashy car, stays late at work.*

5. *Legal problems, process server, sudden flight.*

"It wasn't my fault we had to skip town," said Lexine. "I mean it wasn't my problem. I didn't embezzle that money. Sure, I was with him in Mexico, but when he disappeared for good, what was I supposed to do? I was broke. I came back home." Lexine lifted a slack hand. "Mother's gone. This is my house now."

The rush of words was over. Lexine leaned back in her chair and lit a cigarette.

Homer cleared his throat. It was question time. "Mrs. Dunphy, I wonder if you remember anything about the night you left your house in Cambridge. Do you remember anything about the evening of May 29th? Do you recall what happened across the street?"

"You mean about the baby?"

Homer controlled his excitement. "You saw what happened?"

191

"Not till after. We were all packed up. Jack had this rental truck, wanted to take off in the middle of the night. So we were waiting, watching TV. The TV set belonged to the landlady, so it was still there, along with the rest of her crummy furniture. It must have been between eleven and midnight, because it was Johnny Johnson. He had James Mason on the show, you know, the actor, he's dead now."

"Did you hear something on the street?"

"Right, there was this squeal of brakes. I remember I turned my head." The vertebrae of Lexine's neck were no longer capable of twisting sideways, so she swiveled her whole body to the left. "I didn't get up to look because I was really so interested in the show."

Homer nodded, imagining Johnny's sly questions and the actor's dignified replies.

"But then there were all these screams," said Lexine.

"Screams? What kind of screams?? Was it a child? A woman? A man?"

"A woman. Oh, yes, it was a woman all right. You know, real shrill and high, scream after scream. Well, of course when the screaming started I jumped up and ran to the window. Jack too. We both looked out the window."

Homer said it in a whisper, "What did you see?"

"The dead baby, lying there in the road." Lexine put her head back and blew smoke at the ceiling.

"What else? Who was screaming?"

"The baby's mother, Mrs. Fell. She was climbing out of the car, screaming and screaming. She was drunk."

"How do you know she was drunk?"

"She could hardly stand up. Then her husband got out, he was worse."

"Are you saying, Mrs. Dunphy, that the car that killed

192

the baby was driven by his own parents?"

"His mother. She was the one got out on the driver's side. And then she tried to pick up the baby, only she dropped it. God! And then her husband tried to pick it up, but he tipped over and just lay there, only he wasn't out cold, he was shouting at her. I wanted to yell out the window, but Jack said shut up." The phlegmatic Lexine shook her head in disgust. "So then she got back into the car and drove it into the garage, leaving her husband and the baby lying there on the street."

Homer was bewildered. "But I thought it was the babysitter's fault. The fault of the baby's cousin? That's what the paper said."

"Well, of course it was. That little kid. It must've been her fault for letting him get out of the house. She'd gone off to a dance and left him alone."

"A dance? She went to a dance?"

"Right, I suppose it was this high school dance, like they had one every Friday night. God! Well, then she came sashaying back, hurrying along the sidewalk, just as Mrs. Fell came out of the garage and tried to get her husband to stand up. I mean, the baby was still lying there. I didn't recognize the girl at first because she was all gussied up. You know, her face was all smudged with rouge and lipstick and mascara, and she had on these high heels and sort of a cocktail dress."

"But wasn't she only about twelve years old?"

Lexine stubbed out her cigarette. "Oh, right, but she'd made herself look a lot older. She must have dolled herself up with her aunt's lipstick and so on, and then probably she put the baby to bed and walked out, only he climbed out of his crib and toddled out of the house right into the road. And then a drunk driver came along and ran over him, and it was his own mother."

Homer was speechless.

"It was just so incredible. The mother, she was still screaming. When her niece showed up she flew at her, and her fingernails were stretched out like claws." Lexine's fat fingers raked the air. "She scratched the poor kid's face, so the kid began screaming too and her face was all bloody."

Homer was still stunned.

"I wanted to call the police, but Jack said hell no." Lexine lit another cigarette. "But somebody else must have called them, because a police cruiser came along. And, you know, an ambulance. We didn't want to attract attention, so we turned out all the lights until everything quieted down, and then by three in the morning we were out of there."

Homer staggered to his feet. "Well, thank you, Mrs. Dunphy. I'm so glad to know the truth about the baby's death. It's a big help."

Lexine too struggled up from her chair by pushing down on the table with both hands. "Don't mention it. Have a piece of cake?"

"Oh, thank you, no. You've been very kind." Homer escaped, his mind reeling.

Snakes

All men are at each other's throats.

M.C. Escher

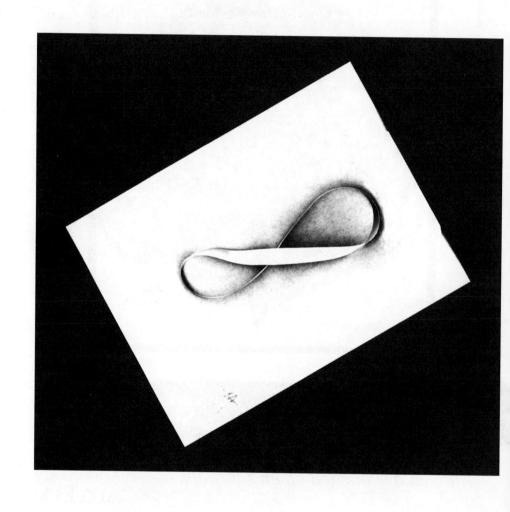

55

THERE WAS A NEW DISPLAY OF HATS IN THE SHOW window of Maud's Twice-Told Togs, the little secondhand boutique on Huron Avenue between the laundry and the gilt-edged grocery store.

The hats had been a great find. It was an entire boxful, unopened since the 1950s. Maud Starr had bought the whole thing for a song from an impoverished old lady milliner. There were pillboxes, toques, beanies, snoods and tiny chapeaus with feathers. Maud had priced them top dollar. They were going like hotcakes.

But right now business was slow. Maud passed the time of day with her friend Sally on the phone, keeping a sharp watch on the passersby on the sidewalk. A lot of women paused to study the hats. One of them excited Maud's interest. She said, "Whoops, Sally, gotta go," and snapped the phone shut.

It was a stranger, a smartly dressed woman in a green coat. Maud watched her gaze at the hats for a moment, then move out of sight.

The coat! Surely it was the very same green coat that had been bought a couple of months ago by an interesting man named Leonard? So interesting that she had followed him up the hill? Since then Maud had tried a couple of other ruses, hoping to snare the guy's attention. So far they had failed.

But here was a possible new connection, the coat. Leonard must have given it to this strikingly handsome woman.

Maud bounded out of the shop, hurried after the woman and pulled at her sleeve. "Oh, excuse me," said Maud. "I couldn't help noticing your coat. I think it was in my shop." She waved at the pretty hats in the window. "I think I sold it, this very coat, a few months ago. Am I right? Did someone give it to you?"

To some people, Maud's aggressive curiosity might have been offensive. To the woman in the green coat, it was not.

She whirled around and gazed eagerly at Maud. "No, but there was another one. They were on sale and I bought two at the same time. I gave one to my niece. Did you get it from her?"

"No, no, I didn't see who brought it in. But I know who bought it and took it away. It was a man."

"A man?" It was Maud's turn to be grasped by the arm. "What man? Did you get his name and address?"

Maud was surprised, but she was delighted to plunge deeper into this fascinating mystery. "Leonard, that's his name. And he lives"—Maud pointed—"just around the corner on Sibley Road. Number 24, an old house at the top of the hill."

Mary and Homer Kelly had once been acquainted with Maud Starr. They had thought of her then as a bird of prey, a vulture, a snake. She was still a snake. Here on the sidewalk on Huron Avenue there were now two coiled and poisonous snakes, swaying their narrow heads and flicking their forked tongues. One was preparing to strike.

56

WHEN THE DOORBELL RANG, ELOISE WINTHROP ROSE slowly from the sofa. She was not feeling at all well, but the thought of a visitor cheered her up.

She was almost too late. Frieda had started down the porch steps when Eloise opened the door.

"Oh, my dear," called Mrs. Winthrop, "do come in."

Frieda turned back, smiling. "Oh, thank you, Mrs. Winthrop. I'm on my way to Mount Auburn, but I couldn't resist stopping by to thank you for the other day."

"Dear child." Mrs. Winthrop fluttered after her into the house. The front hall was dark, but a flicker of sunshine glowed on Zachariah Winthrop and his Zulu warriors. His safari helmet was effulgent. Frieda smiled up at him as she followed her hostess into the sitting room.

"Do sit down." Mrs. Winthrop picked up a blanket from the sofa and tossed it aside. "I'm sorry it's so untidy. I was just having a little nap."

"Oh, did I wake you up, Mrs. Winthrop?"

"No, no." Eloise sat down carefully, while Frieda sank into an upholstered chair across the room. "You're visiting your uncle this morning?"

"Not exactly." Frieda jumped up and dragged a straight chair close to Mrs. Winthrop—there was something about the old lady that invited affection. "I want to climb the tower."

"The tower?"

"The tower of Mount Auburn. Remember, I told you it was like one of the pieces in a chess game?"

Mrs. Winthrop put her hand on her breast, feeling the faint rapid beating of her heart. "A chess game?"

The rook, Mrs. Winthrop, the rook in the Escher print called Metamorphosis, *the little tower on the bridge to the beautiful city.* "Do you play chess, Mrs. Winthrop?"

"Oh, no, dear. Zachariah tried to teach me, but I couldn't understand."

"Well you must have seen the pieces. They have funny royal names. The piece like a horse's head is the knight, the ones with crowns are the king and queen, the little tower is called the rook, or the castle."

"Yes, dear." Mrs. Winthrop's smile was angelic.

Frieda quelled an impulse to kiss her. "Are you going to visit your husband this morning, Mrs. Winthrop? Won't you come with me?"

"Oh, no, dear. Perhaps I'll walk down a little later."

But when the next visitor came to the door and sounded the buzzer, *bzzzt-bzzzt,* two whole hours had gone by. Mrs. Winthrop was still lying quietly under her blanket. With difficulty she heaved herself to her feet and went to the door.

What a surprise! Mrs. Winthrop gasped, "Why, Mrs. Fell!"

Kitty stared at her suspiciously. "I do not believe we have met."

"Well, not really." Mrs. Winthrop giggled. "But in a way we're neighbors. In the cemetery."

Kitty was still frowning, failing to understand.

"Narcissus Path," explained Eloise. "I've often seen you there, Mrs. Fell. My husband's grave is just above you on Willow Avenue." She pointed at the photograph on the wall. "He was a very distinguished anthropologist."

Kitty did not turn her head to look at the picture. She

continued to stare at the dotty old lady. Coldly she said, "I'm looking for Leonard. Is he here?"

"Leonard? Oh, no, I think he's gone out." Mrs. Winthrop knew very well that Leonard had gone out. She had heard his step on the back stair and she had waited with the steaming kettle in her hand, hoping to hear a knock.

There was a pause. Mrs. Winthrop felt a kindly concern for the strain in the woman's face, the nervous twitching of her hands. With natural graciousness she pointed to the precious things in her husband's collection and explained the two-stringed tamrong from Cambodia, the prayer wheel from Nepal, the Kwakiutl totem pole. Then with a heavenly smile she turned back to her visitor and said, "Your little boy. You often visit him."

The animal faces on the totem pole bared their teeth at Kitty. Staring back, she thought of her bitter grudge. "Why, yes. Yes, I do."

"And a young relative of yours comes too, Frieda, such a darling girl, bringing flowers for her uncle's grave."

Kitty woke up. She grasped Mrs. Winthrop's arm and said sharply, "Frieda? You've seen Frieda?"

"Why, yes, dear Frieda. She was here just a minute ago. She stopped by on her way to the cemetery. She wants to climb the tower." Mrs. Winthrop's heart quivered in her breast. "You see, it's like a chess piece. She explained it all to me so nicely, the knights and castles and kings and queens. She said the tower is like the castle."

"Oh, my God." Kitty gaped at Mrs. Winthrop, then whirled and started for the door, stumbling on the tiger rug, grasping at the hookah and falling flat. The hookah crashed to the floor with an echoing clang.

"Oh, my dear, are you hurt?" Mrs. Winthrop helped Kitty up, and said kindly, "I'm going there myself, to visit Zachariah. Won't you share my taxi?" She made a deprecating gesture. "I know it's silly of me. I usually walk because it's so near. But today I think I'll call a cab."

57

ONCE AGAIN THE GOODYEAR BLIMP FLOATED OVER Mount Auburn Cemetery.

"Pretty dull down there today," joked the pilot. "Nobody committing suicide."

"Kind of empty, matter of fact," said the co-pilot, staring down at the paths winding among the spreading canopies of the trees. The spring flowering time was over, giving way to the fresh green leaves and emerald lawns of early summer. "Where is everybody?"

"Weekday today. Everybody's at work."

"Nice afternoon though. Hey, there's a taxi. Imagine taking a cab to visit a tombstone."

"You got anybody dead yet?"

"Me? Heck, no, I'm only twenty-two." The co-pilot kidded the pilot. "You're an old guy. How about you?"

"Oh, sure, my grandparents. Memorial Day, that's when we go. Pay our respects once a year."

It was true that the burgeoning garden of Mount Auburn was nearly empty of visitors on this lovely afternoon in late June. But a bunch of children from a day camp trailed after their counselor along Cypress Avenue and gathered around the sphinx. An amateur photographer wandered along Central Avenue, looking for interesting graves. He snapped the tower of boulders dedicated to the memory of Brigadier General Jones and stared into his viewfinder at the marble dog guarding the Harnden monument. Near Halcyon Lake a birdwatcher knelt in the bushes. He had heard a report of a peregrine falcon. His binoculars were at the ready.

And two women came in a cab. They were Eloise Winthrop and Kitty Fell. While Eloise paid the driver, Kitty took off, galloping up Central Avenue.

Mrs. Winthrop called after her, "Oh, Mrs. Fell, do you know the way to the tower?"

Kitty merely loped up the hill, panting. She did not turn her head.

Mrs. Winthrop looked after her, a little disconcerted. There had been something strange in her companion's fierce silence in the taxi, and now there was something even stranger in her lunging ascent of the hill. She was pursuing her niece, that charming young woman called Frieda.

Walking slowly along Beech Avenue, Mrs. Winthrop could not stop wondering about it.

Settled at last in her comfortable encampment beside Zach's grave, she lifted her face to the exquisite summer air and closed her eyes.

When she opened them again, she was stretched out flat on the grass. Why, she must have dozed off for a minute. Turning on her side, she could see straight down the little hill—past the azaleas, past the trunk of the beech tree, past baby Patrick's grave—all the way down to Narcissus Path, where she was not surprised to see her tenant pacing up and down.

She called to him, "Leonard, dear."

His white face looked up at her in a dream. Slowly he

climbed the little hill, following the procession of black-clothed mourners who were carrying their small casket on their bowed shoulders. When they swept silently past Mrs. Winthrop, Leonard stopped and bent over her.

Her face was ashen. She sat up and leaned against her husband's tall stone, her hand on the front of her dress. "Leonard, you told me—"

Leonard knelt in front of her. "Yes, Mrs. Winthrop?"

"You told me you were interested in that nice girl—" Mrs. Winthrop paused, looking puzzled.

"In Frieda? Yes, yes, I am."

Her attention strayed. "Oh, look, dear, there's the peacock."

Leonard glanced at the long dark shape stalking past the Lowell monument in the direction of Oxalis Path. The peacock moved like a chicken, jerking its head and pecking at the ground.

Mrs. Winthrop had been thrown off course. Wistfully she said, "I wish it would—"

Leonard was not interested in the peacock. "Mrs. Winthrop," he said urgently, "you were talking about Frieda."

"Oh, yes, of course. Forgive me." Mrs. Winthrop clapped her hands feebly. "She's here. She's on her way to the tower."

Leonard was thunderstruck. He started up and stared wildly at the treetops rising to the south.

"Wait, wait." Mrs. Winthrop crouched lower against her husband's gravestone. She was gasping for breath. "Her aunt—"

"What? Her aunt? Go on, Mrs. Winthrop, go on." Leonard reached out and took her hand. The poor old lady looked so ill. "Mrs. Winthrop, are you all right?"

She looked up at him with a smile. It was the same

smile that had won the heart of Zachariah Winthrop, so long ago. "Oh, yes, dear, I'm quite all right." But then her expression changed to a look of alarm. "Leonard, I think you should—it's Mrs. Fell, you see. Frieda's aunt is following her, and I think perhaps—"

Leonard turned away and began to run. At once the dark procession blocked his way. The long parade of mourners was taking its time crossing Willow Avenue. He had never seen so many marchers in the solemn parade, so many crouching figures ascending and descending, going around and around.

He was confused. Which way had he been going? The veiled woman at the head of the procession was turning back, she was looking directly at him. He could see her eyes through the black haze of her veil. She was beckoning with her black-gloved hand.

At once it was clear to Leonard that she knew the way. Gladly he nodded and followed her, becoming part of the procession. She walked ahead of him, her veil lifting and flowing, the men bearing the casket plodding soundlessly behind him, their black shoes rising and falling. Around they went, around and down, then around and up again.

It was a Moebius strip of course, he should have guessed it before. Oxalis Path along the shore of the lake twisted once on the way up to Willow Avenue, then flowed smoothly around and around.

There was no escape. Leonard marched uneasily, trying to remember what it was that he had been trying to do. They went around once, twice, three times. They were parading along the shore of Auburn Lake for the fourth time when Leonard heard someone call his name.

58

"WHY, MR. BATES, YOU STARTLED ME."

It was Barnabas Bates, the founder of cheap postage. "Letter for you, Mrs. Winthrop," he said politely, holding out a creamy envelope.

"Why, thank you, Mr. Bates."

"Invitation to a garden party," confided Mr. Bates, slapping his bulging leather bag. "She's invited everybody."

"Who has, Mr. Bates?" said Mrs. Winthrop, eagerly opening the envelope and slipping out the pretty card.

"Mrs. Gardner. Down there on the lawn in front of her place. You know, beside Auburn Lake. You'd better hurry, Mrs. Winthrop. They've already lighted the Japanese lanterns." Mr. Bates strode away to deliver more invitations. Over his shoulder he called back something about *triangular sandwiches.*

Yes, yes, the invitation was for this very afternoon. If she didn't hurry, she'd be late.

Mrs. Winthrop struggled to her feet and made her way across the first half of the loop of Willow Avenue, and then the other. Oxalis Path was steep, but already she could hear the happy sounds of the garden party. Cautiously she made her way down, clinging to twigs and branches.

At the bottom she stopped to take a shaky breath and calm her racing heart. It was so exciting! There was the little stone bridge across Auburn Lake, and there was Mrs. Gardner herself on the other side, her long skirt trailing on the grass. She was holding out both hands.

"Welcome, my dear," called Mrs. Gardner, laughing.

"Welcome to the other side."

Overjoyed, Eloise hurried across the bridge. The party was in her honor! Gently Mrs. Gardner took her arm and introduced her to the other guests. "Mrs. Winthrop, have you met Mr. Longfellow? Do you know Mrs. Farmer? Oh, Fanny, dear, your triangular sandwiches are so delicious."

Eloise was entranced. The Japanese lanterns glowed orange and pink, green and blue. Mary Baker Eddy was there at one side, holding court in a crowd of men and women, all beautifully dressed. One was Senator Sumner, so handsome and youthful in his black frock coat. And look, there was Harold Edgerton snapping pictures, his flash bulbs sparkling on and off. And oh, someone was bowing to her! Mrs. Winthrop beamed at Joshua Stetson as he swept off his ten-gallon hat.

So many guests! They were all talking cheerfully, holding their delicate teacups and nibbling at their sandwiches. Near the wide-open door of the Gardner mausoleum stood Buckminster Fuller, cracking jokes with Oliver Wendell Holmes. And who was that handsome officer in blue? Surely it was Robert Gould Shaw? Even the Mountforts were there, so charmingly triangular. What a splendid gathering of distinguished and important people!

And then to her astonishment Mrs. Winthrop saw a familiar person on the other side of the lake.

It was Leonard. There he was again, right there on the other side of the bridge, looking at her doubtfully.

Oh, but he must join them. He must come to the party. He must be one of them, here on the other side.

"Leonard," cried Eloise, "cross the bridge! Leonard, dear, cross the bridge!"

She saw him hesitate, but then her attention was

distracted by the peacock. How delightful! It was poking through the shrubbery and strutting among the guests, the perfect final touch to this most perfect of all garden parties.

Smiling with joy, fainting and dying, Eloise dropped to her knees. But Zach was coming, striding across the grass, stooping to embrace her.

And look! Look at the peacock! It was spreading its tail in a splendid fan of green and gold. At last!

And therefore Mrs. Winthrop did not see Leonard tear himself away from the procession of mourners and race across the bridge. She did not see a second Leonard, a backwards reflected Leonard, brush roughly past him.

Leonard was free. The Escher transformations had all reversed themselves, the spiral whirlpools had gushed the other way, the double mirror had released him and engulfed his spectral twin, the endless staircase had sprung a trapdoor, the imprisoning crystal had been smashed—and the ends of the two-dimensional miracle that Frieda had called bewitched, the Moebius strip, had flown apart.

Their two fantasies—Leonard's and Mrs. Winthrop's—had mingled into one.

59

FRIEDA STOOD ON THE PARAPET AT THE TOP OF THE tower on Mount Auburn's highest hill. Around and below her the green hills and valleys were dotted with graves. Beyond the encircling road a pair of obelisks rose narrow and tall. Above her hovered the Goodyear blimp, voyaging in the mild soft air.

She was not interested in the near landscape. Her eyes gathered in the entire horizon, the whole broad view of the city of Cambridge and the high-rise buildings of Boston. Far across the rooftops the white steeple of Harvard's Memorial Church was a fragile spike beside the solid tower of Memorial Hall. To the south rose the pretty domes of the river houses, but the Charles itself was invisible, flowing between the two cities.

Somewhere in the middle distance lay her own neighborhood. Yes, there was City Hall, and those blank glassy shapes must be Kendall Square, and beyond Kendall the squat dome of M. I. T. looked old-fashioned and snug among the high techno-rises. Was that glint of gold far away across the river the dome of the State House? Probably not, but the gleaming pillar standing all alone to the southeast was certainly the glassy shaft of the Hancock building, higher than anything else.

Frieda smiled with delight. She had been right. She had walked into the print called *Metamorphosis*. This fat round tower was like the rook on Escher's chessboard, the playing piece that was also a stronghold, a fortress belonging to his charming city.

Kitty was exhausted. Her old bones balked, her feet staggered. The winding stone stairs were cruel. Again and again she stopped to rest, panting for breath, leaning against the curving wall. Again and again she pulled herself grimly together and carried on, because Frieda was there, she was up there on the topmost level of the tower, she was cornered. Kitty had seen her from far below staring straight out to the south, gazing at the view.

Why was it so much harder than the last time? Kitty had not been quite so old the last time, when she had climbed these very stairs in the company of that wretched geologist, after luring him here with her lying letter, the one she had cobbled up so cleverly from a library book. Of course it was too bad the poor man had turned out to be the wrong Leonard, but was that her fault? It was not! The blame was entirely Frieda's. *Frieda's again, Frieda's again.*

This time, climbing these twisting stairs, she felt a hundred years old. But it wouldn't take long, it would be over soon, it would be quick, very quick, and then she'd lie down. *Only a moment, and she could lie down.*

At the top of the stairs Kitty waited in the open door, letting her anger restore her breath. There before her was Frieda, right there within easy reach, thin and small. Frieda's back was turned, she was leaning against the railing, she was half over the edge already.

An easy target! *Quick, quick!* A convulsion of bitterness spewed from a thousand pockets of sorrow, and Kitty lunged at Frieda, wrapped her arms around her and hitched her, hoisted her, heaved her up off the stone floor. *Quick, quick, now, quick!*

She had the advantage of surprise. Frieda struggled and cried out, but her arms were pinned and when she struck backwards with her feet they battered against legs that were columns of brass. Overbalanced on the railing, Frieda screamed. She was staring straight down at the paved road.

And then she wasn't. She cried out in pain as she was scraped roughly backward and thrown down. Whimpering, she looked up to see Leonard Sheldrake drag Aunt Kitty back from the parapet. Kitty was shrieking and flailing and trying to wrench herself free. Frieda jumped up and caught at a kicking leg. Leonard lost his balance and fell backward.

210

At once Kitty slithered sideways and sprang up on the parapet and lay down on its thick stone teeth. They were deliciously soft under her green coat.

After all, what did it matter? Oh, sleep, she would sleep and sleep.

There were shouts of warning. People looked up, they were crying out.

Smiling, Kitty rolled over ever so gently and fell into empty air.

60

"JESUS," GASPED THE PILOT OF THE BLIMP, LOOKING down.

"God almighty," cried the copilot, "it's happened again."

Leonard and Frieda leaned over the parapet and looked down. They could see only a circle of backs bending over Kitty. There were hushed exclamations of distress. A man stood up, took something from his pocket, tapped it, and held it to his ear.

"The green coat," said Leonard, stepping back, gripping Frieda's arm and drawing her away from the railing. "It was hers, the other green coat."

"Yes, of course." Frieda spoke in a dream. "Of course it was her green coat." There were pounding footsteps on the stairs, and she was looking at him critically. "I remember now," said Frieda. "When I tried to draw your face I forgot what your hair was like."

Leonard pawed at his hair, pleased to find it parted in the old way. And his watch had jumped from his left wrist to his right.

People were bursting out on the platform. "Jesus God," said the first one, gaping at Leonard and Frieda. A dozen more excited witnesses came pelting after him through the door.

The last was the amateur photographer, lugging his tripod and satchel of cameras. It turned out to be his lucky day. That evening the *Boston Globe* paid for his picture of six people bending over the dead woman at the foot of the tower and they also paid for the crazy print of a couple of happy-looking witnesses at the top.

"They kept laughing," he said, accepting the check. "It was really strange."

The high spirits of Leonard and Frieda were indeed strange, but no one accused them of pushing the woman off the tower. To the people looking up from below, the poor lady's intention had been clear. "Nobody pushed her. She climbed up on that parapet by herself. And then she just sort of rolled over."

61

LEONARD'S APARTMENT WAS NOT A PERFECT REFUGE from the downpour that flailed at the windows and drummed on the roof. Some of the rain streamed from the hole in the ceiling and rattled into the bucket on the floor.

They sat around the bucket in a circle—Leonard and Frieda on the edge of the bed, Homer on the stool at Leonard's desk, Mary on the sagging upholstered chair.

"She was a pusher," said Homer. "Not drugs, of course. Pushers like Kitty Fell must be fairly common because it leaves no evidence. And it's so easy."

212

Mary shoved at the air. "Just a little nudge on the edge of a cliff."

"That's right," said Leonard. "You don't need a handgun or poison or an explosive device. Not even a piece of string around the neck. All it takes is a little push."

"You know," said Frieda slowly, "Tom fell too. My husband, he fell too."

"Your husband?" said Mary.

Leonard put an arm around Frieda, but she jumped up and clenched her fists. "I know she did it. I knew it all the time. Tom fell off the platform at Harvard Square in front of a subway train. The woman who was driving the train thought he'd been pushed, but nobody else saw anything. Everybody crowded around while they picked him up, and Aunt Kitty must have hurried away up the stairs."

"Were you there?" said Mary doubtfully, "How can you be sure?"

"Well, of course I can't be sure. But she'd been so angry when I told her I'd married Tom. She shrieked at me about what I'd done to her, reminding me about Patrick, as though I could ever forget. And as though I could ever forget what she said to me then, that I'd never—she said I'd never have a child of my own." Frieda clasped her hands in anguish. Leonard pulled her back down beside him and held her close, but she had something else to say. "So when this happened, I nearly went crazy. I screamed at her, *Where were you?*"

"Well, where was she?" murmured Homer.

"Oh, she had an alibi," said Frieda bitterly. "She said she was visiting Uncle Edward in the nursing home. But when I called there, the head nurse said she was pretty sure he'd had no visitors that day."

There was a stunned silence. Then Homer said, "Hey, Leonard, watch it, the bucket."

It was full to the top. Leonard leaped up, Frieda ran to the cupboard and found a saucepan. Leonard slid the bucket sideways, Frieda shot the pan into place, Leonard dumped the bucket in the sink, Frieda slid the pan deftly out of the way and Leonard put back the bucket. The stream of water thinned. The rain had stopped.

Homer laughed. "Hey, talk about teamwork."

Mary clapped her hands and gushed, "Why don't you two be little friends?"

"Good idea," said Frieda.

"Brilliant," said Leonard. "I never would have thought of it myself." They sat down grinning, their arms around each other.

"Let's see now," said Homer. "Where were we before this act of heroism?"

Mary pulled herself up from the sunken cushion of her chair. "You know, Frieda, there's something we've been confused about from the beginning, the names. We've had them all mixed up. Poor old lovesick Leonard didn't even know your last name. It's Field, right? Your husband was Tom Field? Good, then what about your maiden name? Was it Fell?"

"No, no. My mother was Uncle Edward's sister. She was Margaret Fell before she married my father, Henry Clover." Frieda laughed ruefully. "Tom and I liked the way Clover went with Field. I was Frieda Clover Field."

"It'll be Sheldrake, as of next week," said Leonard, putting in a cheerful claim. "Scheldrachi in Uzbek. It's a kind of duck."

"Quack," said Frieda politely.

"A duck, of course," said Homer. "Quack, quack. But

214

Frieda dear"—he hitched his stool forward—"would you mind telling us something about that creepy aunt of yours? She had all of us so completely baffled."

"Oh, of course we figured out some of it," said Mary, "when we learned she'd changed her physical appearance. But it was really so mystifying, the way she claimed to be Edward's niece instead of his wife. Well, we know now that she was your Aunt Kitty, but the name she gave at the nursing home was Eleanor Fell. What was her real name, Eleanor or Kitty?"

Frieda sighed. "She was both. My aunt's name was Eleanor Catherine Fell. The Kitty came from Catherine."

"Oh, of course." Mary groaned. "And there was an O in there somewhere, wasn't there? O for Oliphant, in honor of her glorious ancestors?"

"Oh, it was so insane. The Oliphants were supposed to be descended from royalty. I forget which royalty. Dukes and duchesses anyway."

It was time to go. "There's just one more thing I don't understand," said Homer, getting to his feet. "How did your Aunt Kitty get so rich? Where did that hundred thousand come from, the money she gave to the nursing home?"

Frieda shrugged her shoulders. "I guess she inherited it from Uncle Edward. I think it was all tied up in trusts until he died." Sadly Frieda whispered, "Poor old Uncle Edward."

Awkwardly Homer changed the subject. "Leonard, what's going to happen to this great old house? I suppose Mrs. Winthrop's executor will have to sell it?"

"I wish we could afford to buy it," said Mary.

"It's already on the market," said Leonard. "Listen. You hear that?" There were bumping and crashing noises downstairs. He went to the window and looked out. "The moving van's here."

"Hey, watch it," said the guy at one end of Mrs. Winthrop's sofa as they edged it through the front door. "I think a leg just fell off."

"I'll pick it up later," said the other guy. "Creeps, she sure had a lot of stuff."

"Now, listen to me, you people," said a man in a tweed jacket, looking on with disapproval, "remember what I told you. You're not to touch anything in the front hall. Not one single thing."

There was a vibrating crash as his butterfingered colleague dropped the hookah from Morocco, denting it for the second time. "Whoops," said the colleague, glancing guiltily at his partner.

The other anthropologist merely picked up the hookah and said comfortingly, "Who's to know?" And then the two of them bowed inquisitively over the tamrong from Cambodia, while Zachariah Winthrop looked mildly down from the wall and made no complaint.

The movers were nearly done when the burly manager of the moving company found an envelope on the dainty little desk in Mrs. Winthrop's bedroom. The envelope was stamped and sealed and addressed to—

Michael J. Rooney
100 Court Street
Boston Massachusetts
02108

"What the hell are we supposed to do with that?" said his assistant, looking over his boss's shoulder.

216

"Mail it of course," said the manager. "It's got a stamp, right?" He thrust the letter into his pocket, hoisted the desk and carried it out under his arm.

Unlike other impossible and insane pieces of correspondence, this one was real. It was a letter from the grave.

62

"HOMER," SAID MARY, SLINGING HER BAG OVER HER shoulder and plunging down the porch steps, "I'm off to see Barbara."

Homer was standing on the bottom step, looking out at the water. "Barbara? Oh, right. In the nursing home."

"It's such a hot day. I'm going to push her wheelchair around under the trees in the cemetery."

"Well, good for you. Listen, Mary." Homer caught her by the sleeve. He had something important to say. "I don't want to move to Cambridge."

Mary laughed. "You don't want to move to Cambridge? Well, that's settled then." She brushed her hands together, sweeping away the dust of Cambridge. "We'll stay put."

"A contractor," said Homer happily, "I'll hire a contractor to fix the driveway and lower the gradient. Going up and down will be easy as pie."

It was a decisive and singular moment. They were back where they started. Somehow they had safely negotiated the erratic twist celebrated by August Moebius, descendant of Martin Luther, author of *De Computandis Occultationibus Fixarum per Planetas,* an astronomer whose fame reached as far as the moon, where a crater bore his name.

In Mount Auburn Cemetery Mary swooped Barbara's wheelchair up and down the avenues and paths. They whisked along Halcyon Avenue past the round temple marking the grave of Mary Baker Eddy, and on Central Avenue they paused at the Harnden monument to admire the faithful dog. At the fork with Chapel Avenue they looked up at Nathaniel Bowditch, sitting so comfortably above them with his great book on his knee.

The flush of summer flowers was over. At the junction of Pine and Cypress beside the sphinx a couple of groundskeepers were setting out chrysanthemums.

It was cool in the leafy shade. Mary reminded Barbara that the trees in the cemetery had never been attacked by men with chainsaws. No one had ever lopped away branches to prevent interference with wires suspended between telephone poles, because there were no wires, there were no poles.

They wandered this way and that among the clusters of memorials, admiring the way each gravestone was appropriate to the fashion of its time. There were obelisks, gothic steeples, classical temples, urns, boulders, columns, Celtic crosses and varieties of angels. Some of the angels blew silent horns, some held torches rightside-up, some upside-down. Most of the angels had wings, some didn't.

"They're not angels, I'll bet," said Barbara, gazing at a marble lady who held one arm aloft, pointing skyward. "The ones without wings. They're allegorical figures."

"Noble abstractions, I guess," said Mary. "You know, like death or eternal life or grief. This one's telling us that somebody named"—she squinted at the inscription—"John Tyler—is not down there under the ground, he's up in heaven."

218

Then Mary whirled Barbara's wheelchair around and rolled her briskly downhill, because it occurred to her with dismay that this mortuary perambulation might be hard on her crippled friend. Perhaps Barbara was thinking gloomily about her own death.

She was relieved when Barbara said cheerfully, "It's really nice here. Let's come back."

They left by the Egyptian gate, while ninety-thousand voices murmured behind them from the stone memorials—from the polished sphere and the triangle and the octahedron and the balancing cube, from the obelisks and angels—

We were like you. We were all of us just like you.

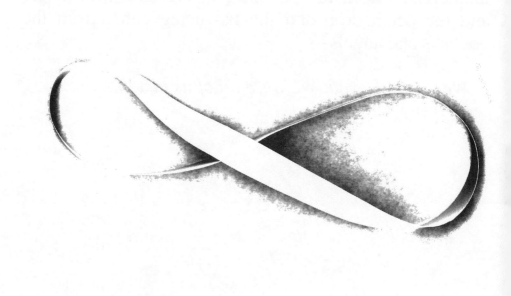

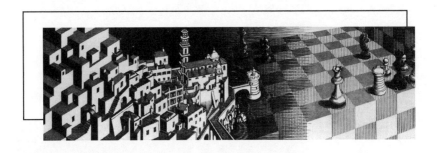

Metamorphosis

The blocks give rise to a city on the sea-shore.
The tower standing in the water is at the same time
A piece in a game of chess . . .

M.C. Escher

63

THE CITY OF CAMBRIDGE HAD SURVIVED A TWIST OF ITS own. There had been a transit strike. There was popular indignation at the city council's refusal to reduce taxes for the elderly. The head of the Cambridge Building Department had been hauled before the State Ethics Commission. Gentrification was creeping in all directions. There were lavish improvements to properties in Mrs. Winthrop's neighborhood—Brattle and Lakeview, Sibley and Fayerweather, Appleton and Sparks.

But not to Mrs. Winthrop's property, because on a lovely September afternoon during the last week of her life Eloise had written a codicil to her will, properly witnessed by her cleaning woman and the man who came to read the meter.

The consequence of her last act was that Leonard, checking on her mail one morning as he did every day, found a letter from her executor. It was not like the bills he had been forwarding to her accountant. It was addressed to Leonard himself.

He read it three times before he understood the central paragraph—

I leave my house and all its contents to Leonard Sheldrake, in gratitude for his kindness to me and his appreciation of the work of my husband Zachariah.

Signed by:　　　　　　　　*Witnessed by:*

Eloise Creech Winthrop　　*Galatea Stokes*

　　　　　　　　　　　　Joseph P. Malone

"Oh, Mrs. Winthrop," whispered Leonard, "I don't deserve it." He unlocked the front door and stood gazing around the empty hall, which still spoke so eloquently of his gentle landlady. There was a dark patch on the faded grasscloth where Zachariah had once looked down so benevolently from the wall, and a light patch on the floor where the tigerskin rug had so recently bared its fangs. "I wasn't kind to you at all, dear Mrs. Winthrop, I wasn't nearly kind enough."

Burdened with a monstrous feeling of guilt, Leonard abandoned his plans for the afternoon and rocketed into Boston on the T. At the Park Street station he bounded up the stairs and dodged through the crowds on Tremont Street, arriving out of breath at the corner of Court Street, where he found his way at last to the office of the executor. Plunging past the secretary in the outer office, he apologized to the astonished executor and fiercely disclaimed any right to deprive Mrs. Winthrop's heirs of their inheritance.

The executor looked at him mildly. "As it happens, Mr. Sheldrake, there was only one previous heir, the Anthropological Society of America. I have already informed the president of the society that all Mrs. Winthrop's furniture is to be removed from storage and returned to the house."

In a daze, Leonard had the presence of mind to ask, "But what about the totem pole and the tamrong and the hookah? What about the picture of Professor Winthrop? Surely they don't have to give all those things back?"

"Indeed they do," said the executor primly. He did not unfold to Leonard the painful scenes of the last few days—the outrage of the anthropologists and his own courageous and adamantine resistance.

Leonard left the executor's office in a state of dazzled

confusion. In a telephone booth on Tremont Street he called Frieda and told her the staggering news.

"Oh, Leonard," she said in horror, "think of the taxes, how will we ever manage?" Then before he could answer, she said wildly, "The attic! We'll rent out the attic! We'll take in lodgers! A whole houseful of lodgers!"

Mrs. Winthrop's was not the only will that was a dumbfounding surprise to its legatee. Mrs. Kitty Fell left everything to a distant second cousin once removed, a woman she had never met, a retired school teacher who possessed the single virtue that she was not, never had been, nor ever would be a little bitch named Frieda.

Frieda neither knew nor cared. She and Leonard were too busy trying to settle down in their inherited real estate. It wasn't easy. Mrs. Winthrop's house was so large and complex, they sometimes lost touch with each other. Leonard would shout, "Where are you?" and Frieda would cry from somewhere far away. "I don't know. Try heading north."

Well, of course it was M. C. Escher all over again. It was his upside-down and inside-out staircases, his scrambled perspectives. But it was no longer one of his crystals. Leonard had given up on crystalline perfection in an attempt to adjust to the happy-go-lucky ways of his wife, who was a lot more into chaos than order. Leonard's worktable was no longer a study in parallelograms and right angles. It was a comfortable shambles.

So was the back yard. To the owners of the house next door their overgrown garden was an offense. The neighbors had spent a fortune on a glass conservatory with an ogee roof like a cathedral—*our premier model with the soaring elegance of a palm house*—and another

225

fortune on a fashionable landscape gardener. Therefore it was an affront to look over their clipped hedges at the careless wilderness next door, the back yard once so cheerfully neglected by Mrs. Winthrop.

Eloise herself was past caring about the neighbors. She had moved to another neighborhood entirely, more beautiful by far, where at last she could lie cozily beside her husband Zachariah.

Mary was glad about Frieda's and Leonard's good fortune. Sentimentally she said to Homer—once again bringing the end neatly back to the beginning—"Maybe love at first sight works out sometimes after all. Tell me, Homer, did you fall in love with me at first sight?"

Mary was just kidding, but Homer said flatly, "Yes, I did."

"Oh, well, of course, so did I. Fall in love with you, I mean. You were the first man I'd ever met who was tall enough." She laughed. "Think of it, all these years of ecstasy."

"Ecstasy? Well, maybe." Homer thought it over. "I'd call it more of an ecstatic interminable squabble."

"Oh, of course." Mary thought a minute. "An everlasting amorous wrangle."

"A grouchy perpetual passion." Homer snatched up the thesaurus.

"Oh, good," said Mary. "Let's try both categories."

They spent the next half hour, true scholars that they were, trying to define the precise nature of their affection, combining Roget's category 795, synonyms for DISACCORD, with 931, words signifying LOVE.

226

Afterword

IN THIS BOOK THE MAP OF CAMBRIDGE HAS BEEN stretched to include a fictional Sibley Road between Lakeview Avenue and Fayerweather Street. The gallery and the shops on Huron Avenue are inventions too, as is the burial plot of the Fell family at Mount Auburn Cemetery and the monument marking the resting place of Zachariah Winthrop. Other gravestones are genuine, including those of Joshua Stetson and Barnabas Bates. As of this writing the peacock is also a fact, an anonymous contribution to the wildlife of Mount Auburn.

Thanks are enthusiastically due to Meg Winslow, Curator of Historical Collections at Mount Auburn, to Janet Heywood, director of Interpretive Programs, and to David Barnett, Director of Operations and Horticulture. Of course they are not to blame for the fictional events set in their beautiful garden.

Others who helped the story along are geologist Gretchen Eckhardt, Cambridge residents Chris Weller, Maury Feld and Marian Parry, Attorney Judy Pickett of Littleton, Doctor Joel Feldman of Mount Auburn Hospital, John and Anna Miller of the Psychic Connection in Boston, Detective Sergeant Joseph McSweeney of the Cambridge Police Department and the other members of his team, Detectives Brian Branley, James Dwyer and John Fulkerson.

I'm also greatly indebted to Professor Arthur Loeb

and his wife Lotje, who were friends of Maurits Escher in the Netherlands and also his hosts in Cambridge.

Most of all I'm grateful for a correspondence with my son Chris about mirror reflections, singly and doubly twisted Moebius strips, mysterious reversals, the stacking of cannon balls, topological twists and knots, crystal lattices and the dilemma of the chameleon in the mirrored box. A big help too has been the warm encouragement of his brothers Andrew and David, longtime fans of the prints of M. C. Escher.

His work teaches us that the most perfect surrealism is latent in reality . . .

—Albert Flocon

Dear Reader:

I hope you enjoyed reading this Large Print mystery. If you are interested in reading other Beeler Large Print Mystery titles or any other Beeler Large Print titles, ask your librarian or write to me at

Thomas T. Beeler, *Publisher*
Post Office Box 659
Hampton Falls, New Hampshire 03844

You can also call me at 1-800-818-7574 and I will send you my latest catalogue.

Audrey Lesko chooses the titles I publish in Large Print. Our aim is to provide good books by outstanding authors—books we both enjoyed reading and liked well enough to want to share. We warmly welcome any suggestions for new titles and authors.

Sincerely,